MINILUV

Rebecca Suter
2021

RealMatter Publishing

CONTENTS

ONE.

A woman in her twenties walks out of a grey building wrapped in a grey jacket, hugging herself against the wind. Her black hair is short and thick, shiny like crow feathers; her lean body moves swiftly through the crowd, blending with its flow. She is not beautiful, but something in her catches the eye; a hint of lust in her brisk steps, a soft sway of the narrow hips that speaks of worlds far away from these grimy buildings. A smile ripples her face for a fraction of a second. She looks straight ahead and walks, fast and furious.

Soon she reaches the entrance of the Ministry of Truth, a massive steel door carved inside the three-hundred-meter-tall pyramid of white concrete. As she enters the building, a middle-aged man in a trench coat approaches her, opens his mouth as if to speak; her pupils dilate in fear. The man seems to change his mind, closes his mouth; she hurries on and blends with the crowd, thousands of identical employees marching in unison towards thousands of identical offices. The pyramid sucks her in, and she lets herself be swallowed.

At her workstation in the Fiction Department, Julia positions herself between two sets of metal levers and begins to manoeuvre them, pushing buttons on the board in front of her. A combination of word processor and printing system, the machine composes texts and produces multiple unbound copies of cheap novels for the proles. From there an operator picks them up and hand-carries them to a device that binds them together with colour pictures, unrelated to the content, often but not always of young women with large breasts and skimpy dresses, or equally scantily clad pretty young men.

Every five minutes Julia chooses ten words to initiate the composition process, introducing an element of randomness that no software, however sophisticated, has so far been able to generate. Ten new words for each book; she types them in, pushes a green button, and the machine creates a medium-length novel based on a series of sentences containing those ten words. This takes about sixty seconds. For the next four minutes, Julia moves the levers to ensure that the printer works in sync with the computer, calibrating its rhythm. During this phase, the novel machine operators also proofread the final product. Long strings of words appear on a screen set in front of each worker. They proceed very quickly; typos and mistakes are left in. The only thing they need to check is that the machine does not produce completely meaningless texts, for instance repeating the same sentence for pages on end, which happens sometimes. In that case they press a red button to stop the printing and start over.

Julia's body moves inside the machine with perfect rhythm and speed; she is one with the metal gears, the levers an extension of her limbs. Around her, eleven more operators dance in their eleven identical steel cages, the metal thumping and clanging. They work in this fashion for five hours, from seven hundred to twelve hundred; at noon a bell rings and all operators stop at once. The machines slow down and stop, spitting out the last unbound copies. Cooling metal slates make little popping noises.

Julia is the first to get out of her steel and silicon cage. She is already at the door, taking off her green scrub with one hand and pulling a Victory tobacco pouch and a packet of rolling papers out of her overalls with the other hand, when the telescreen bloats, "Comrade Unwhite! Report to the Planning and Development Office of the Fiction Department immediately!" Panic flickers in her eye for a fraction of a second. She walks out at an even pace, not towards the canteen but in the opposite direction, down the dimly lit corridor.

She enters a room, closes the door gently behind herself, then rushes to the desk where a man is sitting in a black leather chair, not looking up from his papers. She puts both palms on the desk and leans in on him, trembling with fury. After several seconds the man looks up at her, seemingly surprised to find this thing on his desk, a fuming young woman.

"What are you, crazy? What possessed you to approach me in the foyer this morning? Do you want to get us both killed?" she whispers, then turns quickly around, and sighs in relief. The telescreen is turned off, its lucid dark surface showing only a tiny desk, a tiny Julia, and a tiny man on a tiny leather chair. The man stares at her for a while, not speaking. Then he sighs; his eyes soften and suddenly he looks fragile, older. "I'm sorry. You're right. It was a silly thing to do."

"Much good it does me, to be right." She sighs, too. "What is it, then? What's so important that you need to summon me to your office in the middle of the workday? Thank god you Inner Party people can turn telescreens off whenever you like. And by the way, how many minutes do we have before you have to turn it back on?"

"Five minutes."

"Sounds damn short to me."

"Julia, I did not ask you to come here to have sex, for heaven's sake."

"You did not exactly *ask* me to come here, if I may say."

"Sure, you're right, again. I'm sorry I had to do it that way. But we don't have time to discuss this now, I hope you understand it. We only have a few minutes left, and we need to talk."

"About?"

"We cannot go on like this, Julia. I'm sure you realize it yourself. It's too risky, and it's not good for you either. You are a bright, beautiful young woman, and you should be with someone who gives you what you deserve. You should get married, you know. The Party would appreciate that."

"Michael." He flinches and she smiles; calling him by his first name between these walls feels almost like a crime. It probably is, one of the thousand things you don't even know are illegal, but that you are supposed to understand you should not do. It feels forbidden, naughty, exciting. Julia has a hunch that her lover likes it too, the thrill and threat of it. "Michael, we discussed this a hundred times, why is it so urgent now? Why tell me in your office, in the middle of the day? And besides, you know it's all bullshit. You say we should break up almost every time I see you, and next thing you know you're taking off your pants."

"Exactly, and that's why I wanted to talk to you here, in full daylight, in the office. Because we really must..." he breaks off, then resumes his speech, no longer shy or pleading. "Comrade Unwhite, we have to discontinue our encounters. Which, in fact, never happened."

"What the fuck, Michael..."

"And that will be all, comrade Unwhite. On behalf of the Fiction Department Project Control Board, let me thank you for your report on the productivity of the Ultimate Printing Endeavour. The Control Board appreciates your leadership in service. You can join our comrades in the canteen now."

The slight buzzing sound and the monotone female voice reading lists of figures behind her back alerts Julia that she is not allowed a reply. "The production of boots has tripled this month; rations of chocolate will be raised to twenty grams per week." Once a telescreen is broadcasting, its receiving function is turned on as well; the two cannot be separated. Talking screen, spying screen. All Julia can do is perform her best incinerating stare, making sure that her back is turned towards the telescreen. To no avail; the man is immersed in his papers, careful not to meet her eyes. "Thank you, comrade O'Brien. It is my pleasure to serve the Party to the best of my abilities." She walks towards the door and bows briskly before closing it behind herself.

TWO.

Early morning. Winter is almost over, yet cold gusts still sweep the streets, lifting scraps of paper and brown leaves. The light from the lampposts makes the high rises look flat and unreal, like cardboard figures. Julia walks fast, hair tousled by the wind, bare neck exposed. A flat smile on her lips, her eyes intent yet calm, her face is a smooth, efficient mask; it has no openings.

The time is just before six hundred and the streets are empty. A door opens; an old man in grey pyjamas puts a bulky vinyl bag on the pavement and goes back inside. A rat runs across the road and disappears into the gutter. Julia walks on; she finally stops at the front door of one of the high rises. The building looks like all the others: twenty stories, grey walls, rows of rectangular windows reflecting the grey sky. She knocks lightly on the door: no answer. She tries the knob, and it opens.

Inside is a grocery store, a large room partitioned by walls of shelves. The place is spacious, it hosts some fifty rows of shelves; about half of them are empty, while others hold only a few unlabelled cans, covered in dust. On the remaining shelves are mostly dry goods: rice, oats, sugar, tea, coffee; at the far end of the shop a few lines of tinned beans, spam, and chocolate. The label-less cans and boxes are neatly stacked and arranged in a rational, functional way. A row of shelves is devoted to toiletries, and it is the emptiest of all. A few bars of grey unscented soap, a few bottles of Victory Cologne, and an impressive number of blue and red plastic toothbrushes—there must be a few hundreds.

Julia walks through the aisles and stops in front of the chocolate shelf. There's only one type of chocolate, wrapped in foil, a dozen identical bars. She takes one, weighs it in her hand, smells it, feels the texture by squeezing it softly between her thumb and her index finger, and repeats the operation with each bar. Finally, she settles for one, sniffs it again to double-check, and walks to the cashier. A red-haired woman with thin metal glasses raises her eyes and looks at her blankly.

"Good morning comrade, I would like to buy this bar of chocolate, please."

"Ration card, please."

"Oh, yes, wait..." She fumbles in her bag for a long time; the redhead keeps staring in silence, until Julia produces a small booklet with a blue faux-leather cover.

"I'm sorry, comrade, but this is not valid. You cannot have your chocolate ration for the month of February unless you update your ration card."

"I beg your pardon?"

"Your card needs to be updated. You cannot buy chocolate with this card."

"But this expires next year, see? It says on the end page... valid until January 1985. Look."

"I do see it, comrade; nevertheless, your card needs to be updated. The Party issued a new type of card at the beginning of this month, which means that you need to either get a new card, or you have the old one stamped and updated. I cannot sell you anything with this card."

"Couldn't you make an exception? Like, just for this once? I'll get the card renewed today, tomorrow at the latest. No one needs to know. I have an awfully busy week and I won't be able to come again to the shop before the end of the month, so I will miss my ration for February... if you could... just for this once... I won't tell anyone, I swear..."

"I'm sorry, comrade. Your card is not valid. You cannot purchase your chocolate ration for the month unless you get your card updated."

A flash of anger runs through Julia's forehead, but the Flat Smile quickly smooths down her features.

"I understand. Thank you for the information. Do you happen to know where I can get my card renewed or stamped? Could you tell me where I should go, if that's not too much trouble?"

"You have to ask the relevant office, comrade."

"Right, of course. Would that be in the Ministry of Plenty, do you reckon? Or should I ask the Ministry of Truth first, since they handle all ID cards? If you would be so kind as to tell me who I should ask…"

"As I said, you have to ask the relevant office."

"Of course. Thank you so much. You were really helpful."

"You are welcome, comrade. On behalf of Victory Stores, I thank you for choosing to shop at our venues, and I wish you a pleasant day."

A flurry of wind makes Julia's scarf fly as she exits the store; she runs after it and catches it just before it falls in a frosted puddle in the middle of the road. She wraps it around her neck, unwraps it, and rewraps it around her head. Thick raindrops begin to fall, leaving coin-sized dark spots on the tarmac. It is now six hundred ten; work begins at seven hundred thirty. The Ministries are all in the city centre, yet each building is a few blocks long, and it can take a long time to get from one to the other even for a fast walker like Julia. And once you are inside a ministerial office, no one knows how long it will take to get out of it. But a whole month without chocolate feels utterly unbearable. And it's not just the chocolate; if they don't update my card it's a fucking big deal. Your ration card is your life: gin, tobacco, sugar, pens, paper. And thank god I don't shave, but it is the only way you can get razor blades too.

Off she goes, in the opposite direction from Minitrue and on to Miniplenty.

THREE.

The Ministry of Plenty is possibly the bleakest among London's government buildings. Tall and unadorned, it doesn't have the grandeur of the Ministry of Truth pyramid or the essential, minimalist style of the windowless Ministry of Love. It is just made up of several run-down high rises, connected to each other by bridges located at the fourth and seventh floor level, and by paved pathways inscribing the courtyard with dull geometrical patterns. The buildings are numbered, one to twelve, with big black characters painted on the side and repeated in a smaller font on the main door.

On the ground floor of building number seven, a metal banner with neatly painted red letters says "Enquiries." Inside there's a single desk behind a glass wall; at the desk sits a chubby man in his fifties, with sand-coloured hair and bluish white skin. Enter Julia, smiling her flat smile.

"Good morning, comrade, I was wondering whether you could help me…"

The man does not give any sign of noticing her.

"… there seems to be a problem with my ration card, I don't know which office I should talk to in order to fix it, apparently they changed all cards last month, and now one needs to have it updated, or so they tell me. I'm not sure which office deals with this?"

"This is the enquiries office. We do not issue documents."

"Sorry. Let me rephrase this. I am Julia Unwhite, from Ficdep in Minitrue, and I need some information. I wonder if you can help me."

"What information do you need, comrade Unwhite?"

"Could you tell me which office handles the update of ration cards?"

"You need to go to office 324A, in the Mungo Malungo Building."

"Say what? I mean, could you spell that for me?"

"M-u-n-g-o, M-a-l-u-n-g-o, B-u-i-l-d-i-n-g."

"Thank you, comrade, I appreciate your help. Have a good day."

As soon as she exits the building, Julia realizes that she forgot to ask which building number is Mungo Malungo; she walks towards the map in the middle of the courtyard, but sure enough it only lists the buildings' numbers and not their names.

Dreading another conversation with Sandy Hair, Julia decides to try buildings at random, hoping to hit Mungo Malungo in a reasonable number of attempts. As luck would have it, she finds it at the second try: it is building number nine. An almost identical flaxen-haired chubby man is sitting behind what looks like an old school desk. This one, though, is a bit more animated; he greets Julia with a smile and actually speaks to her first.

"Good morning comrade, how can I help you today?"

"I'm looking for room 324A, do you know where I should go?"

"Room 324A, let me check this for you, here, it's on the eleventh floor."

"Are you sure? I mean, if there's any logic to the building, why would room 324 be on the... never mind. Eleventh, you said?"

"That is correct. If you walk down that corridor and make a left, you will find the elevator right in front of you. I'm afraid it's out of service, though."

"Thank you, comrade. I like to take the stairs anyway. Get a bit of a workout."

Slightly out of breath, Julia arrives on the eleventh floor and walks down the dark corridor. Room 320, 321, 322, 323A, 323B, 324B, 325. Wait. 323B... 324B. 326, 327A, 327B... the corridor makes a sharp angle, a new row of doors: 401, 402A, 402B. Julia retraces her steps, turns right: room 311, 312, 313... After walking around for ten minutes, she finally finds room 324A, a tiny door squeezed between 718 and 719A. She knocks and enters. Another pudgy blond guy is sitting at the counter.

Either they have a policy about hiring triplets or there is some weird cloning stuff going on at Miniplenty. Oh well. Better not think too much about it.

"Good morning comrade, your colleague downstairs sent me here, I hope this is the right office. I need to update my ration card." Julia takes out the booklet and puts it on the desk, still holding it with one hand. The man reaches for it; she instinctively grabs it tighter, then she lets go with a nervous laughter.

"But your card expires in January 1985, comrade. You can only renew a document three months before its expiry date."

"Well, that's what I thought too, but today I went to buy my monthly ration of chocolate and the woman at the shop refused to serve me, saying that I need to update my card. It seems that they issued a new type of ration card last month, and all the old ones need some kind of stamp to be valid."

"We only issue cards, we don't update them; and we can only issue a new card up to three months before the expiry date."

"Yes, you said that, but... well, could you perhaps tell me who should I contact to have mine updated, then? Which office handles this?"

"This is beyond my competence, comrade; all I can suggest is that you consult the New Guidelines on Rationing, issued by Miniplenty on February 4th."

"And do you happen to have a copy of the guidelines?"

"Unfortunately, they are currently out of print; you might find a copy in the National Archives."

"But don't you have a copy in the Ministry? I mean,

if this is where the document was originally issued, certainly you must have…"

"I'm afraid we cannot allow customers to consult internal documents; the access is restricted to employees of the Department of Rationing, Inner Party Members, and researchers with regular special permission, stamped by the relevant authority."

"But this is not a fucking *internal* document, it's a manual for all citizens, right? If I can consult the copy that is at the Archives, then why not the one you have here?"

"I would appreciate if you toned down your language, comrade. In any event, I do not have a copy of the guidelines myself, so I'm afraid I cannot help you."

"Look, I am a member of the Ministry of Truth; can the request be passed on to them? My supervisors can vouch for me, I'm sure."

"I'm afraid we cannot do that; it would account to intra-ministerial interference, which, as I am sure I don't need to remind you, is punishable by law."

"Of course. I understand. Thank you for your assistance, comrade."

"It is our pleasure to serve the public, comrade Unwhite. Thank you for your time. Have a productive day."

This is turning into a nightmare. And since O'Brien has dumped me, I have no longer access to Inner Party chocolate rations either. Or gin, or coffee, tobacco for that matter. Walking at her usual brisk pace, Julia makes her way to Minitrue, praying that her delay will not cause further trouble.

FOUR.

Thumping, clanking, wheezing, the novel-writing machines work at full speed, spitting sheaths of paper, warm and smelling of fresh ink. The rattle is so loud that it takes a few moments for anyone to notice that an insistent, imperious message has replaced the monotone listing of this month's production statistics coming from the telescreen.

"Comrade Unwhite, report to the Personnel Office of the Ministry immediately!"

The voice blares out the sentence several times before Julia finally notices. Her work mates exchange the briefest of looks, too quick for the telescreen to register, but slow enough to let Julia know that her being singled out twice in less than a month has not gone unnoticed. Is she suspected of conspiracy? Is she an Inner Party spy? Either way, she's trouble. Eyes locked on their machines, the men and women's shoulders speak contempt and fear. The nail that sticks out gets hammered down. Do not mess with it or you'll be in trouble too.

What can this be about, and more importantly, where the fuck is the Personnel Office? I bet it's about the ration card. I shouldn't have asked to have this referred to Minitrue. What if the Miniplenty employee reported me for attempted interference with the course of bureaucracy? Or could it be O'Brien who ratted me out? Or that guy I was sleeping with before, what was his name again? I have such a shitty memory. O' Shea? O' Whatshisname, was he in the PO? Nah, that was ages ago and anyway it was before they renamed the office. So is it about the ration card then? Calm down, Julia. Calm down.

Wiping her oily hands on her overalls, Julia approaches a grey metal door, and knocks on it with a resolve that betrays her unease.

"Come in, comrade."

"Julia Unwhite, identity number 27121975. I was summoned by the PO a few minutes ago."

"That is correct, Comrade Unwhite. Apologies for disturbing you during working hours. I hope this will not affect your productivity, with which the department is much impressed, as we are with your overall performance, may I add. It is very unfortunate that Minplenty has had to reject your request to update your ration card. We were notified of your request and found the situation most regrettable."

So the guy did dob me in after all. Shit. Play your cards well, Julia. Forget the chocolate, the chocolate's no problem. I already missed the February deadline anyway. Play your cards well, Julia...

"As you know, here at the Ministry of Truth we take our personnel development very seriously. I am sure you are aware that you might incur heavy sanctions for attempting to interfere with the course of bureaucracy. However, there are alternative arrangements that could be undertaken."

Ha. The pig. Thank you O'Brien, you Inner Party members sure know how to keep a secret, hey? So where do you want to have your alternative arrangements? This desk looks pretty damn uncomfortable, if you ask me. Julia stands still in front of the desk, arms resting at her sides, releasing the tension from her shoulders, flat smile firmly in place.

"The PO of Minitrue has recently entered a new pilot program, part of a larger development scheme that will be eventually scaled up to a whole-of-Oceania approach. Based on your achievements in the Ministry as well as your success in community and industry engagement, you have been selected by the executive committee to be part of the pilot. Comrade O' Brien would be your direct supervisor. Participating in the pilot would automatically allow you to qualify for promotion to Level B Step 6. Your performance review would also, of course, be passed by default."

Huh?

"This is a very delicate task, involving a high level of responsibility and secrecy. You do have the option of not accepting. In that case, your request to update your card will be rejected, and you will have to resubmit it once the standard waiting period has elapsed, which, if I remember correctly, is twelve months in this case. Since this is a rather urgent matter, I will need your answer immediately."

"I am honoured by the offer, Comrade. It is my duty to serve the Party to the best of my capacities. Thank you for considering me for this position. When will I receive further details?"

"Very soon, Comrade. Very soon."

FIVE.

Monday morning, nine hundred fifty eight. In the offices of Minitrue, workers are rushing down the corridors, streams of green scrubs and blue overalls converging in a bigger flow headed towards an open door. The Two Minutes Hate is about to begin; most employees are already sitting with straight backs and expectant eyes in front of the big telescreen on the back wall. In their haste no one notices Julia and O'Brien as they exit his office together and join the crowd. They separate as they reach the rows of chairs, without looking at each other. O' Brien takes a seat next to a small sandy-haired woman; next to the woman is a skinny man with fair hair and rough red skin. Julia sits in the row behind, the scarlet sash of the Junior Anti-Sex League tight around her hips, her back straight, the usual blank look upon her face.

At eleven hundred, a piercing noise fills the room; the Two Minute Hate has begun. The face of Immanuel Goldstein, the former leader of the opposition, now Enemy of the People, fills the telescreen. As she tries to suppress a smirk, Julia's face contorts ever so slightly, as if she could not bear the sight of the man's wrinkly face, his short beard, his long thin nose, his downy white hair. As Goldstein starts pouring a flurry of venomous and overly simplistic insults on Big Brother, the Party, and the whole of Oceania, Eurasian troops appear on the screen behind him, marching in their identical uniforms and identical faces, like a single body, a perfect machine, frightening and fascinating. Immediately people begin to murmur, angrily, first in whispers, then more loudly, until the entire room starts roaring; people jump off of their seats, their shrieks covering Goldstein's bleating and the thump of the soldiers' boots. Julia gets up from her chair, yelling: "Swine!" She picks up a Newspeak dictionary, that she had left for this purpose under her chair, and flings it towards the screen. She stands, staring at the man's pixelated eyes, clenching her fists, shaking all over. She's a maniac.

Taking their cue, everyone stands up, looking at the screen, trembling with rage. Just as Big Brother's face appears on screen, calm and powerful, overwhelming and soothing, Julia quickly turns towards the red-skinned young man. She is looking at her, as she sensed he was. His gaze frightens her and fills her with a strange excitement. After a second, the flash of intelligence in the man's eyes is gone, his face turns dull like everyone else's, pacified, defeated. Julia does not dare try to catch his eye again; their locking gazes was too serendipitous to be repeated, at least in the same session. She can only hope that their brief interaction has not been captured by the telescreens, and that it has not escaped her direct supervisor's atten-tion. The first contact has been made. Pilot Project E-999 has begun.

SIX.

Eleven hundred. I think I am drunk. And how nice it is. Victory Gin is so disgusting, oily and flavourless and stinging, it brings tears to your eyes and warm joy to your brain. Unfocused. It is so lovely to be unfocused. Everything falls into place, or perhaps it does not, but that's ok too. All is good; I feel these are the only moments when I am truly myself, when I am true to my self. The body softens up and so does the mind. Both life and death feel easier to deal with somehow. Colors more vivid, joints looser. A deep sense of peace, a calm vibration, wells up from the centre of my body. I gulp down one more glass, feel the heat in my throat spread to my stomach and from there to my soul.

I needed the booze top up after tonight anyway. Too many strange things happening. And all because I went to the Marlborough Pub. It was a reckless thing to do, especially now that I am working for the Inner Party and they are very likely watching me even more closely than others. But somehow I always feel I have a margin, that I can afford to break rules as long as I am careful, that my good girl persona will protect me. I hope I'm not being stupidly overconfident. I hope I'm not heading towards disaster. I have this feeling sometimes that I will be found out and my castle of deception will crumble over me, leaving me bleeding and bewildered.

I got a real scare tonight when I saw a Thought Police guy at the far end of the counter, but he was just there having a drink by himself, perhaps eyeing the girls, or the boys, anyhow I'm pretty sure that he was completely uninterested in me. I sat at my usual spot, in the middle of the right-hand side of the U-shaped counter, in front of the beer taps. Jim was at his table in the opposite corner, with a schooner of dark ale in front of him. Alone. Like he knew. Perhaps he did.

I sat there with my Victory gin, dying to look at him, staring ahead. Even in prole pubs, Party members only get Victory gin, which tastes like petrol and probably contains quite a bit of it too. Proles have beer, which is supposedly inferior yet looks so terribly inviting, all frothy and cool, tears of condensation dripping down the glass, tracing the contours of my envy.

Jim was drinking his beer in little sips, like he always does, like a girl. Sober in a room of drunks, smiling his knowing smile. We sat like that for a while. In the seats between us, two tall guys were having a heated argument, swaying their hands in front of each other's bloated faces, shiny with sweat. The policeman stared at them nervously, uncertain whether he should pretend not to see, or intervene. Brawls among the proles are tolerated and even encouraged, as a simple letout that pacifies them. In the stuff we produce at Ficdep, gang fights are second only to pornography in popularity. But it's a fine line between a drunken fight and that little bit more that could result in actual trouble, and the policeman knew it.

Jim seemed to be in no hurry, to the point that I started worrying that he might not have seen me, or, worse still, might have lost interest. More than the blow to my pride, the thought of the missed opportunity would have hurt me for days. But finally he stood up and made for the door, leaving a few copper coins on the table. I waited five minutes and followed him outside; he was waiting for me three blocks down to the left, two to the right. So reliable. He does not want to get caught any more than I do, after all.

SEVEN.

A fine drizzle begins to fall, soft tiny drops in the darkness. Julia and her lover walk in silence, he following her about ten metres behind. One after the other, they turn into a dark alley and walk through a tall wooden door leading into a courtyard. The cobblestone is dark and shiny, slippery with dampness and grease. The air smells like mould and soap and frying oil. Wafts of vinegared fried fish overpower the other smells, then subside again. The two climb the dark stairs in the far left corner; she slows down and he speeds up, and they reach the last flight together. The stairs open onto a roof where a few damp sheets hang from rusty wires. Jim takes them down and piles them up in a corner; "Are you sure this is ok?" asks Julia. "They will get dirty, they're not even ours."

"They'll wash them again. Lie down. I'll make you a castle."

Here comes the rain again; big drops on their clothes as they undress, on their bare faces and arms and legs. Flashes of neon light reveal white bluish skin covered in goose bumps, hair slick with water. Proles don't shave their pubic hair like Party members do; the glimpses of the glossy curls between Jim's legs excites Julia. She slides both hands behind his lower back and tugs his pelvis towards hers. "Not so fast, young lady," he laughs. Holding her by the waist with one arm, he turns her to face away from him, and strokes her buttocks with his other hand, parting her legs. Julia kneels on the wet sheets as he enters her from behind, rubbing her nipples. Trying to be quiet intensifies the pleasure; unspoken moans turn into muscular spasms turn into vibrating senses. As they move faster Julia's knees slip under her, her feet get tangled in the soaked fabric, and she falls flat on her face, water splashing around. Pain mixes with pleasure, rain mixes with sweat, tears, and other bodily fluids.

Exhausted, they lie side by side on the lump of damp clothes, suddenly aware of the sound of the rain, drumming drops on different surfaces, a metal sheet here, a mud pool there. Raindrops on their hot faces, in their eyes, in their mouths, water everywhere. Jim tries to stand up and falls back on his butt, feet tangled in his pants. "Slippery when wet," he laughs. "You give love a bad name," Julia laughs with him, feeling light-headed, slipping into another world. Life feels good, if just for a moment. Why does life feel so good, and why always for just a moment?

The rain stops and the sky starts clearing up. Julia and Jim shiver in their wet clothes, yet they don't want to leave. The night is very quiet and very still. The air feels good after the rain, washed, new. Jim is the first to speak, his voice husky from smoking and the cold. "This bloke came to the hotel tonight, before you arrived. I think he was one of your crowd. Maybe they're spying on you, haha."

"You mean a party member?"

"Looks like it, yeah. Blue overalls 'n all. And he talked funny like you do."

"I don't speak like a party member! What are you talking about?"

"Come on, you do, princess. Nothing to be ashamed of. I like it when you talk like a comrade. Turns me on."

"Yeah, right. So did this guy turn you on as well?"

"Nope, hahaha. Don't think so. He was pretty odd though. If he's a friend of yours you should tell him to watch out. Lucky thing he left before the flicks came, but even so, people were staring. He kept asking questions to poor Jack, would not leave him alone. And the old drunk of course would not stop chatting. It was pretty funny."

"What sort of questions was he asking?"

"All sorts of shit. Just really odd."

"Like what?"

"Why do you care so much? He a friend of yours or sumthin'?"

"How would I know? I'm just curious. He might be a spy."

"Who, that one? I doubt it. He was just an idiot. Maybe he was a bit off too, that's why he and Jack got along so well, hahaha."

"Was he asking about other party members going to the pub?"

"Oh, man. No. No, he wasn't. Julia, can you stop being paranoid? You're getting it all wrong. He was not a spy, I'm telling you. You wanna know what he was asking about? Ok, let's see. First, guy tries to buy Jack a beer and acts all nice and friendly, like he has an old men fetish or something. So old Jack orders a pint of beer."

"A what?"

"A pint. Apparently, it's something they sold in the old days, a medium-size beer, between a schooner and a litre. Dunno. But old Jack was damn serious about it; he wanted his pint. Said a schooner's too small and a liter makes him go to the loo in a second. He started talking about his bladder. Your friend was getting all nervous when he mentioned his bladder running. Clearly not his cup of tea."

"He's not my friend!"

"Yeah, yeah, whatever. Not your friend. Your comrade, yeah? Oh come on Julia, I'm joking, ok? Don't make that face. I know you're making a face. It's dark but I can feel it. Listen, it gets better. You're gonna like this one."

She punches him on a shoulder, her fist sinking into the wet wool of his jacket, then laughs and sighs. She wants to hear the rest. She is both worried and amused. She needs to hear this to the end.

"So the guy gets all formal and says, 'you must have seen great changes since you were a young man.'

The way he said it, Jules. You should have heard him. Like he was some theatre actor. Jack starts looking at the toilet door like he wants to run away from this weirdo, and then he goes, well the beer was cheaper, for sure. But Blue Overalls won't let go. He starts this whole shtick about how Jack must have lived before the Revolution, and how was life then, is it true what they tell us in history books, is life really better now than it was then. Whether people were really starving and walking around in their bare feet in the snow, and whether the capitalists really wore top hats and drank champagne."

"Ha. I always wondered about the top hats. In our schoolbooks the capitalists always have these shiny silk hats, and big fat bellies. They must have been pretty unattractive. Those hats look even sillier than our overalls!"

"Funny you mention that, 'cause Jack got really excited about the top hat too. You guys must have something in common huh? Maybe next time you should try to make friends with him. Buy him a pint."

"Oh Jim you are hilarious! I am amazed at your sense of humour!"

Jim punches her on the shoulder, making a squishy sound, and pulls a strand of her shiny black hair.

"Ouch! Stop it! So what about the top hat?"

"Well, he said he used to wear one too, he wore it at his sister-in-law's funeral, like fifty years ago. It was hired, he said."

"Ha! So they were not the capitalists' uniform after all? Wonder if they were funerary apparel. Man, what they feed us in those history books is so much bull-shit. We will just never find out what things were really like."

"Well, I'm afraid you will have to ask Jacko your-self, 'cause Blue Overalls could care less about the top hat. He kept asking about all sorts of shit from those textbooks of yours, whether this and that was true, but Jack had no idea what he was talking about, and went on and on about his memories, how much bet-ter life it was in his youth, and how his bladder can't hold a drop and how he has not gotten laid in ages. Clearly that's not what the guy was after. God knows what he was after. Probably just trouble! It was like two deaf people talking to each other. It was hilari-ous, I'm telling you. Then Blue Overalls got pissed off and left. That was like a few minutes before you ar-rived. You sure you don't know the guy? It was almost like you were taking on from him."

Julia sits up, struck by a sudden thought. She looks at her watch, trying to make out the time in the dim light from the surrounding buildings.

"Do you have to go? What time is it anyway? And why can't you take that damn thing off your wrist at least when we are fucking? It does not seem too much to ask…"

"What difference does it make? I need to keep my watch on. I am a party member. You know that. But no, I still have a few minutes. I was just thinking…"

"Oh, were you? Careful not to overdo it, you might get tired."

"Ha, ha. Listen, what did the guy look like? Maybe I

do know him."

"Very Anglo. Classic party member. Dunno, they kinda all look the same, don't they? Tall, lanky, stooping shoulders, bit of a potbelly. Blond hair, red skin. Sad face. Your typical Blue Overalls guy."

"Anything that stood out? Did he have green eyes?"

"I don't really look men in the eyes, hun. Especially not party members. Had a couple bad experiences already."

"Did he have a briefcase?"

"I think he did, yes. Oh yes, wait, he had one on the table. I noticed cause it was just like yours, you know the one you take from work sometimes. Ugly black fake leather thingie."

"Did it look exactly like mine?"

"Yeah, actually, it was really similar, that's why I thought there was something going on. But then again you guys all have the same uniforms too."

"He must be from Minitrue. I wonder..."

Julia looks at her wristwatch again and stands up. "Gotta go, Jimmy. It's getting late. It was lovely to see you."

"Ditto, baby. Stay out of trouble."

"I'll try."

EIGHT.

Julia walks fast in the cold night, retracing her steps towards the pub. The alleys are pitch black, but she marches on without hesitation; she knows her way too well. And it's getting late. Then she suddenly stops, in a narrow street with a few dark little shops mixed in with prole houses. Even though it's nearly twenty-one hours, one of the shops is still open, its window lit up by a faint oil lamp. Julia stops at the corner and peeps inside; an old man with thick eyeglasses is talking to a younger blond man. The young one has his back towards her, yet he seems somehow familiar. After a few minutes, the man comes out of the door, holding a small bundle in his hands, tenderly, as if it were a living creature. He walks away from where Julia is standing. She starts following him. Could he be...? As if he had remembered something, the man turns abruptly and starts walking back. It is too sudden to move out of his way; their eyes meet. Even in the dim light of the street-lamps, there is no mistaking him. It's Red Face, her target. Was he following her? Is she following him? Is this just a coincidence? He stares back with the look of a lamb on its way to the slaughterhouse. Feeling bold and confused, Julia stands still, holding his gaze. He has, indeed, green eyes. It is only a moment; then the man walks heavily away in yet another direction, pretending not to have recognized her. Julia unwraps her soaked scarf and rewraps it around her neck, burying her face in it, smelling wet wool.

Five hundred and wide awake. I had the strangest dream; the guy with bad skin was in it. I walked through a moorland suffused by golden light. I walked in a straight line across a barren field; the air felt like summer, a late summer evening, balmy with a tinge of chill. I walked on; I knew I could not stop. There was no-one around, not even birds; nothing to see, but the emptiness was beautiful, quiet and vibrant. And at the opposite end of the field, next to a line of elm trees, I saw Red Face. I walked closer and pulled at the zipper of my overalls; they came apart at the seams. As I threw them on the ground, the field disappeared, and I was left in a soft grey nothingness. I woke up.

They told me to monitor my dreams and report on them, so I wrote about that one in the weekly report. It felt strange to write about it, especially the bit about getting naked, even though nothing else happened. I have no idea why they want to know about dreams. I have dutifully reported them, even making up some stuff, sex stuff, subtle though, so that it would not look made up. But they didn't seem to care. This dream, though, they were more interested. Not that they told me why. Probably they're just perving. They get off on it. Well I hope they do, and that it means they keep me on the project, because so far I have had little else to report. In real life, I have not been too successful in approaching Red Face so far. Michael is not pushing me, but I'm worried that his patience will reach its limit soon. It was going so well at the beginning, so many lucky coincidences, I felt it would be a matter of days before I made actual contact. But then, nothing. It's probably my fault too. I don't know what is wrong with me; I hesitate. I may have bitten more than I can chew. I don't know if I can deliver on this.

During the Two Minute Hate the other day, I tried to make eye contact again, but he averted his eyes and looked at Michael instead. For a second I feared he might be cleverer than we think, and that he had figured out there was some ploy to approach him. But that cannot be. He's not that smart. He doesn't look smart. Maybe he's just in love with O' Brien. Fancy that! I don't get him. I really don't know. It's so frustrating. I will try again today; there must be some way. He is a man after all; I know how to handle those.

It is the middle of the morning, and the corridors of the Fiction Department are empty and quiet under bright neon lights. Julia is walking back from the infirmary, at her usual fast pace, looking straight ahead, one arm in a sling; an injury from the novel-making machine, too light to grant her any days off. At the far end of the corridor, she sees a blond lanky man walking toward her. When they are a few metres apart, she kicks a leg back and falls forward, flat on her injured arm. She winces and turns pale, pain flashing through her elbow. The man rushes forward, helps her get back on her feet. As she gets up, hanging on his arm, she turns her back to the closest telescreen and slips a rolled-up piece of paper into his hand. There is a note scribbled on the piece of paper.

The note says: I love you.

NINE.

Sitting alone in a quiet corner in the cafeteria of the Ministry of Truth, Julia suddenly spots the red-faced guy approaching with his lunch tray. Her heart starts racing; but a couple metres away from where she's sitting, he is intercepted by a fat short guy and goes to sit at another table with him. Even without looking, Julia can sense O' Brien's disapproving expression, from the watchtower in the middle of the canteen. What was I supposed to do? Drag him away from his colleague? Why can't you Inner Party guys lend a hand here? I don't even know what I'm doing, or why I'm doing it. Or, well, I do know why: it's the same reason why I do everything. It's because I have no choice.

The next day, however, Julia is in luck: as one of her team-mates from the Fiction Department approaches the table where she is once again sitting by herself, he slips and falls on the floor, his tray flying in the air and spraying grey porridge and gravy all around. In the ensuing confusion, Winston manages to sit right next to her. For a few seconds, they are alone. Now her heart is really racing. What to do? What to say? She is usually the opposite of shy, but the moment is so loaded with tension and confusion that she cannot open her mouth. It is Winston who speaks first, in a quick whisper, eyeing the telescreen in a way that screams suspicious behaviour, but better not bring that up now, after all he is talking to her! He took the initiative! She is too excited and to terrified to say anything.

"Where can we meet?"

Thank God. He's in. That's all that matters; the rest won't be easy, but she knows the drill.

"Victory Square. Next to the monument. At nineteen hours. But only come near me when I am surrounded by the crowd. I'll give you further instructions then. I hope you have good memory. Eat your porridge now, and don't talk to me anymore until tonight."

At nineteen hundred hours on the dot, Winston is on the edge of Victory Square, eyes peeled on the oversized statue of Big Brother riding an elephant. Julia is nowhere to be seen. He looks fretful, scared. As he begins to walk off, he spots Julia heading towards the elephant. When she reaches the monument, people around her seem to disperse; he stops in his tracks, sweating. After five minutes that feel like ten years, a parade of Eurasian Prisoners Of War suddenly enters the square, prodded by guards with sticks and whips. An excited crowd gathers around them, staring and screaming and spitting in the direction of the captured enemies, and Julia quickly slips by his side. She has regained her cool, and instantly begins to instruct her lover-to-be in sharp whispers.

"Listen carefully. Do you know Paddington station? Just answer yes or no. Don't look at me. Whatever you do don't look at me, just walk a pace or two behind, close enough that you can hear me but not so close that it looks as though we're talking. Look at the prisoners. Look angry and patriotic. So do you? Know the station?"

"Yes."

"There's a train leaving there on Saturday at sixteen hundred fifty, headed West. Take it. Get off at Auburn station. The station has only one exit; turn left and walk for two thousand metres on the dirt road. There are no signs, you will have to calculate the distance somehow. After two thousand metres you will see a gate with the top bar missing, on your right-hand side. Cross it and take the path across a field until you reach a grass-grown lane. To your left you will find a track between bushes; walk on it for about fifteen minutes, until you reach a big dead oak tree all covered in moss. Can you remember all that?"

"Yes."

"I'll come a different way. I will try to be there at eighteen hundred. You may have to wait. Are you sure you will remember everything?'

"Yes."

"Then get away from me as quick as you can."

"Yes."

"Now, Christ!"

Winston tries to move, but the parade of prisoners is still going, and the crowd is thick around them. He stands there as frozen, caught in between the prisoners' hollow eyes and the bystanders' eager ones, shiny with spiteful curiosity. As he tries to make his way between two large prole women, turning his face away from their garlic-and-cabbage breath, he suddenly feels something in his hand. Julia is squeezing it, softly and hastily. Not daring to turn towards her, the man leaves his hand in hers, for a very long five seconds. Then she is gone, the feeling of her calluses lingering on his palm.

Damp drafts from a crack in one of the windows fill the room; the cold makes the grey space feel even bleaker. The Junior Anti-Sex League branch meeting is over, and people begin to stand up, the screech of metal chairs on the floors covering the hum of conversation. A bright-eyed teenage girl in the front row turns back towards Julia and asks her in a shrill, bubbly voice, "So what did you think of the meeting?" Julia's Flat Smile quivers with a hint of stifled annoyance. She is about to respond when another woman comes to her rescue: "Cut the crap, Chippy, comrade Unwhite is one of our longest-standing members, you don't need to recruit *her*! Go talk to some actual newcomers. Make yourself useful for a change." Chippy's face clouds up and she scurries away to the opposite end of the room, where a group of teenagers is chanting "Let's make Capitalism history!"

"Thank you, comrade Morrison. I appreciate your intervening there."

"No worries, mate. Kids these days. It's uplifting to see the enthusiasm, but they don't train them as well as they did in our time. Are you coming to see the public execution this arvo?"

"Unfortunately, I will have to miss that one. I have some work to catch up with at FicDep. Gotta get it all sorted before tomorrow morning or I will miss my production quota for the month."

"Oh come on, it's a Saturday! You should come! I heard it through the grapevine that they will execute more than a hundred prisoners. It's going to be massive. Surely work can wait?"

"I am thankful for the invitation, comrade, but duty comes before everything. I hope you enjoy the executions."

Julia rushes for the back door with her scarlet sash still on, and runs down the road, in the direction of the Ministry of Truth—and the bus station.

One hour later, she is walking through the countryside, bathed in the afternoon sun. The clout of smog that constantly hovers over London has not reached this far, and the place is rich in colours. Blue sky, brownish yellow straw burnt by the snow, green, thin blades of new grass, purple and white crocus. Low oblique sunrays cut wedges of the landscape off from the rest, staining them with gold specks. Julia has been here a couple of times before, but the place feels different today; intensely familiar. Suddenly it dawns on her: it's the setting of her dream, the one in which she saw Red Face and got naked in front of him. The resemblance is so extreme it spooks her; she must have dreamed it because she knew it, but it feels as though she knows it because she dreamed it. Walking towards a clearing in the forest, the feeling of recognition becomes more intense and more eerie. Is she dreaming again? A few moments later, as she stands in front of Winston and pulls at the zipper of her overalls, the heath dissolves in a grey haze.

TEN.

It takes Julia some time to get her eyes accustomed to the flickering in the room. Rotating blades of white and blue light cut through the darkness; the air is filled with a cold smoke but there is no smell of burning; rather, the thick, moist gas emanates a scent reminiscent of talcum powder. She and Winston search each other's faces, lit up by a purple glow, for a sign of reassurance that the other knows what is going on. But neither of them does. As Julia begins to take in the scene, she notices that the room is filled with people, moving their bodies convulsively as they stand very close to each other, occasionally touching. What is happening to them? Could it be the effect of the talcum-scented gas? Is this a trick of the Capitalist Underground that we read about in school? Did BB not eradicate it after all? Or is it a trick of the Thought Police, was the heath not a safe haven after all, have we been captured and brought in for torture? Either way, who are all these other people? And are we all going to be killed?

But the writhing people don't seem to be stemming from suffering; rather, their sweaty faces, now dappled with red and green and yellow, appear ecstatic; their intoxicated eyes shine with excitement. None of them is wearing the Party's mandatory blue overalls, nor the tattered rags of the proles. There is no uniformity to their attire, and yet there is something distinctively similar in all of them, as if they belonged to the same tribe. If they do, certainly it is none of the Eastasian or Eurasian tribes that are pictured in textbooks or appear in the war bulletins on Telescreens.

Silver, slick black, and fluorescent pink and yellow trousers are glued to their bodies, showing every curve yet not impeding their frantic movements; some have only a thin layer of elastic fabric around their chest, while others wear what look like armoured tops with extremely broad shoulders. Many of them are wearing shirts of a luminous blue fabric, like some deep ocean fish. When they open their mouths in laughter, their bared teeth shine blue, as if made of the same material. But the most amazing thing is the hair. Some have shaved heads with geometrical patterns, while others have frizzy puffed up coiffures that stand a good twenty centimetres high on their foreheads. A young girl has the left side of her head cleanly shaven, while on the right side her straight, glossy hair hangs down her back, dyed in stripes of blue and green. On a stand at the back of the room two skinny, tall young men stand next to each other, writhing their bodies and opening their mouths in silent screams; one has a purple curly mane that falls down to his waist, while the other's shoulder-length hair is bright yellow, with a red fringe.

Suddenly and almost at the same time, Julia and Winston realise they are both stark naked. Even though nobody seems to be paying attention to them, their faces flush with embarrassment. On a tall stool next to them they notice two neatly folded silvery bundles; Julia picks one up and hands the other to Winston. They are laminated vinyl jumpsuits, with a black zebra pattern and a silver zip at the front, and there are matching silvery lace-up boots. Julia unfolds her parcel and gestures for Winston to do the same; as she slips into the plasticky material suddenly the room fills with sound, loud thumping mixed with singing, humming, shrieking. She turns to Winston to read the same shock on his face. It's music like she never heard before; the rhythm reminds her of the novel making machines at FicDep, yet with a livelier, captivating beat, and before she realises it Julia's body is moving in sync with the tune, a warm pleasure spreading to her limbs. She leans in towards her companion and shouts in his ear, "Let's dance!"

Sliding on the dance floor feels wonderfully unfamiliar. Julia watches Winston hop awkwardly in front of her, his ribcage showing through the flimsy silver fabric of the jumpsuit, pants tight against his pointy hipbones, and wonders if she seems as out of place as he does in this colourful darkness. She spies the movements of the glitter and neon tribe, trying to imitate them and failing to make sense of them.

But she is swaying to the beat and a blissful feeling radiates from her hips to her hands and feet, an enhanced version of a well-known pleasure. The practiced moves of her work at the novel making machine enter her dance and blend with the music. Suddenly swinging her legs on the dance floor feels wonderfully familiar.

Taking her cue from the other dancers, she slips a hand around Winston's back and pulls him closer, shaking hipbone against shaking hipbone. She can smell the sweat on his neck, his breath sour with Victory gin and canned meat. "Let go! Just have fun!" she shouts in his ear, and she rubs her breasts against his chest; the vinyl makes a squeaky noise audible even under the throbbing loudspeakers. They go on like this for a long time, as song follows song, some banging louder, some softer. Sometimes a tune will make the neon and glitter tribe stop in its tracks and begin to sing along, screaming more than chanting, throwing their arms in the air as if they were at a demonstration. The crowd's energy hits Julia like a wave; it's like the Two Minutes Hate multiplied by a thousand. She tries to join the chant, but she doesn't know the words, she doesn't know the rules; explorers in an alien land, she clings to her companion, and as the beat turns to lust they embrace violently against a wall in a dark corner, struggling out of the squeaky silver vinyl, stumbling and falling on each other's sweaty limbs, not sure if they are having sex or passing out.

A gentle breeze wakes them; the sun is almost gone, the heath a little less golden in the chilly evening air.

"Whoa. How long did we sleep?" asks Winston in a hoarse voice, eyes unfocused.

"Thirty minutes, I think. Looks like someone needed it," laughs Julia. "Better rush now, dear. You go back the same way you came. There will be a train at twenty hundred. Be sure not to miss it."

"Will I see you again?"

"Of course! But not here. Better not use a place more than once. The Party has ears everywhere. Stand in the crowd at the POW parade next Wednesday at seven hundred and wait to the right side of the Revolution Memorial. I will approach you when it's safe to do so, and I will give you instructions on where to meet me next." She swiftly pulls her overalls back on, adjusts the red sash on her waist and disappears between the hazelnut shrubs, the sound of her bouncy steps gradually fading in the distance.

ELEVEN.

Late spring is a busy time at the Ministry of Truth. In the lead-up to Hate Week, everyone must work overtime making flyers, banners, and recordings of chants to be played at the demonstrations. As an executive member of the Junior Anti-Sex League, Julia is also involved in training sessions in primary and secondary schools, conducting marching drills for children and teaching martial songs and choreographies. Children are always the most enthusiastic participants of Hate Week; they learn the chants and practice the movements with a dedication rarely seen for subjects like Party History, Principles of IngSoc, or even sports. Their excitement often spooks their parents, and for good reason: while the main focus of Hate Week is, of course, the outside enemies of Oceania, be it Eastasia or Eurasia, one of the highlights of the event is the Young Infiltrator of the Year Prize Ceremony, where the two children, a boy and a girl, who have discovered and denounced the highest number of counter-revolutionary activists in the country are publicly awarded gold medals (since 1975, gold-painted papier-mâché ones) and a year-long supply of Victory chocolate (since 1980, chocolate-covered Victory cookies, made with oats and containing traces of cardboard). While Young Infiltrators are chosen based on the sheer number of counterrevolutionaries they have helped arrest, there is high prestige associated with denouncing one's own relatives, and commendable children who have discovered traitor parents are occasionally given a special Jury Prize. In the days immediately preceding Hate Week there is always a surge of accusations against parents, as children who had slacked during the year try to score last-minute points.

Since child training activities are conducted during school hours, Julia is given special permission to leave the novel making machine before seventeen hundred, or to arrive after seven hundred. Combined with the unreliability of public transport, this means that it is much easier for her to account for long absences from work, and this gives her much greater leeway than usual. Having to run around London in the muggy weather is no fun, but Julia has always enjoyed the months of May and June and the relative freedom of movement they afford her.

This year, it also means being temporarily relieved of the task of engaging Winston and reporting to O'Brien about the development of Pilot Project E-999. While she is not completely exonerated from the job, it is understood that special conditions apply, and priority should be given to anything relevant to Hate Week. Since Winston has also been working regularly after hours in the Revising History department, they have had few opportunities to meet. It has felt as both a relief and a disappointment. Is she getting attached to him? The guy's not exactly attractive; skinny, bad skin, bad hair. But despite the stooping shoulders there seems to be something unbroken in him, a desperate wish for something more, something better. A hope against hope that things will change.

No wonder they put him under surveillance; he probably is a counterrevolutionary. He seems to have no clue of how or when, but he wants to change the world, this world. How stupid is that? What difference does it make? Maybe it's a generational thing. I hate the system as much as the next girl, but I don't really think it is ever going to change. If I fuck him, if I fuck Jim, if I fuck proles or Inner Party members, it is to bend the rules, to play with them, to do what I want behind their back. Until I get caught; or hoping that I won't. But he has that drive, that obstinate hopeful streak. He doesn't just hope not to get caught; he seems to genuinely believe that a better world is possible. And I find that strangely exciting, which is dangerous. Like, really dangerous. If I fall for this, if I let desire get in the way, then getting caught will not be a matter of if but of when.

The proles, on the other hand, are hardly affected by Hate Week at all. They are not involved in any of the production, and are not drilled for the event, being simply expected to spontaneously attend the demonstrations when they happen. In the poor quarters, the only sign that the biggest Party event of the year is approaching is the rise of bets on who will be chosen as the author of the new Hate Song, and whether the melody for the military march is better than those from previous years. In prole pubs, heated discussions always develop on the topic, that sometimes degenerate into violent fights. In a famous case in the summer of 1981, a brawl between a group of older proles who claimed that no Hate Songs worthy of that name had been produced since 1972, and a group of younger proles who hailed the hit of 1980 as the best Hate Song ever produced, degenerated into a riot that took over the whole of King's Cross for five days, resulting in twelve deaths and more than five hundred injured, and the destruction of several houses.

Prole pubs thus tend to be more crowded and noisier at this time of the year, and that has always made it easier for Julia to hang out there unnoticed. Taking advantage of her relative freedom from work, she usually went out to bars several times a week, picking up young prole men. Over the years she had developed a talent for recognizing the ones who take a hint quickly enough for her to be able to direct them to a quieter meeting spot without attracting the attention of other customers. There is a higher risk in approaching someone new—their inexperience might lead them to make stupid mistakes and get them both caught; or they might not be interested and turn her down, although that has rarely happened. But seeing the same prole too many times is also dangerous: they might freak out and rat on her, or they might become too confident and start making demands. More than anything, they tend to get boring; once the thrill of the seduction is over, Julia usually just loses interest and let them go. The men do not seem to mind, or perhaps they are too wary of the danger of pursuing a party member, too aware of how their places in society separated them, to be bothered to look for her.

Jim is different. Of all the men Julia has picked up in prole pubs over the years, only he has lasted this long. It's hard to tell what it is; his dark skin, his pointy teeth, his dusky laugh, the way he teases her but also seems to understand her, really understand her. Being with Jim is always both exciting and comforting. A welcome change from the constant fluctuation between dullness and panic that is life at the Ministry. In the months leading up to Hate Week of 1984, she sees him several times, and always finds herself coming back for more.

TWELVE.

One balmy June evening, heads spinning from Victory gin and lovemaking, Julia and Jim are lying on the roof of a building in the prole neighbourhood of Kensington. Summer is coming; it is twenty-one hundred and the sky is still full of light. The concrete is warm under their bodies, but the air has a tinge of cold. Wafts of jasmine mix with the smell of vinegared fish; voices of children screaming in the street overlap with the distant sound of military drills, someone shouting sharp orders and hundreds of feet stomping.

"Prole children have such different voices from the children of Party members."

"What do you mean? Kids are kids, Jules. It's not like we are born any different from you guys?"

"Oh, don't take it the wrong way! Of course we are all the same human beings. Come on, you know better than to accuse me of looking down on proles? But it's true though. They sound so different. Like these kids now, they yell, but they yell different.

Listen to them: even when they scream, prole children don't sound menacing. Their shouts are random, scattered. Weak. They're not gentle, but they're not scary either. Those kids I teach, Jimmy, they frighten me. When they shout, they are a legion. Eight years old, skinny as can be, four feet tall if that much, but when they gang up, they're an army. It's powerful. They are powerful. Or maybe they're not, not really. I don't know; but they sound terrifying."

"Maybe you think that because you don't have any of your own."

"Any of my own what?"

"Kids. Have you ever thought of having them?"

"God no. And get a spy in my own home? What are you, crazy?"

"Your 'own home' at the moment you share with fifteen girls, am I right? Come on, how is that better? Wouldn't you trust your own family more than strangers?"

"It's twenty girls actually and no, I wouldn't trust a family more than those girls. I wouldn't trust anyone who is a party member; not my housemates, not a husband, and most definitely not children. At least with those girls, by now I know them, and I know how to handle them. I would love to have a place of my own, but the only available housing types are group dorm or family house, and if those are the only options, then I'm fine where I am. Well, I'm not fine. But I can live with it. I would certainly prefer it to marrying a Party member.

Actually, that's one of the good things about being

in JASL; I can put off marriage indefinitely as long as I'm in the League. If you are over twenty-five and still campaigning against sex, it gives you a certain cache with the new recruits. Looks like you're really devoted to the cause. Sacrificing my natural wish to have a hubby and make babies, I'm such a hero, hahaha."

Julia giggles and wraps her hand around Jim's cock, that goes from soft to half-erect under her touch. He wiggles away from her, laughing too.

"Don't turn me on again and leave me out and dry, you know we need to go soon. It's almost curfew time."

"Fuck curfew time!"

"Like, literally?"

Julia giggles again. "No, you're right, sorry. We can't. Damn curfew time. That might be one good side of living in a family home, I might be able to sneak you in at night."

"You so wouldn't! What about Baby Unwhite, he would snitch on me the moment I get in the door."

"So what, I'd get you in from the window!"

"Ha, ha."

"But actually, jokes apart, I might have some good news on that front."

"What, you pregnant?"

"Would you stop it! Not *that* front. I mean about housing."

"What is it?"

"Well, do you remember that red-faced guy I told you about, my colleague at Minitrue? The one I went with a couple of times?"

"More than a couple of times if I remember, and Jules, I know I'm not the only man in your life, but I don't want to hear bloody *details* about the others, thank you very much? Unless it is to tell me that they have a tiny dick. Which this guy probably does, being a Party member and all."

"Hahaha, hmm, you may be right on that one, but that's not the point, and come on, listen, you will like this."

"Whatever."

"No, really, this is good! So anyway. He has some connections, Red Face, and he found a place, in the prole quarters, in fact it's not that far away from here, where this old guy has an antique shop, like he sells old lamps and fancy paper notebooks and quills and paperweights and shit, and he has a room upstairs from the shop, and Red Face said the guy would rent it out to him, so he and I could use it sometimes in the afternoons."

"Good on him."

"Oh come on, Jimmy! Don't you see? He would give me a set of keys to the place, and once I have that, you and I could use it sometimes too!"

"But do you trust this other guy? Antique man? Who is he?"

"I don't know. I don't trust anyone, to be honest. But Red Face seems to trust him. And after all, what could happen? If the guy rats on us, he implicates himself. Besides, he is a prole, and you people mistrust law enforcement, right? He would not go to the police. Also, what would he do that for? We're paying him. He would lose good money, and he would probably end up in jail too, for collaborating with traitors of the Party."

"I don't know, Jules. To be honest it sounds a bit fishy to me. Why would this guy take such a risk? And I don't feel comfortable coming there either. What if he rats on *us* with Small Willy? It's not worth it. Aren't we good here? Look at the view!"

Julia sits up and gazes at the expanse of the sky, the rooftops and the Thames river shining darkly in the gathering dusk. It is, indeed, a splendid view.

"But wouldn't you like to have sex in a real bed for a change, with a roof over your head, actual pillows? There's a bloody *fireplace* in the room, or at least that's what he told me! We could fall asleep in each other's arms, all warm and cosy..."

"Yeah, that doesn't sound like such a great idea either. Dangerous things happen when you fall asleep."

Julia flinches, and a panicked look briefly clouds her face. Dangerous things happen when you fall asleep...

"What, Jules? What did I say?"

"Nothing. It's nothing, sorry. I think you're being silly, that's all. Dangerous things happen when you are awake too, come on. Life is all about taking the right amount of risk. You know I'm not careless. Anyway, we'll talk about this again. You know I'm stubborn too."

"Oh, that I do know." Jim's warm smile lights up his face.

Julia smiles back, worry lingering in her eyes.

"But now I gotta dash. Poster-making meeting at JASL from twenty-two hundred. Fun fun fun."

"Take care, kid."

"You too, Jimmy. See you soon."

"You bet."

THIRTEEN.

On a late June evening, Julia is lying on a double bed in a sparely furnished room, light filtering from the half-closed curtains as they sway in the breeze. The air smells of rain to come, yet the sky seems clear, and what could be mistaken for distant thunder she knows to be explosions from the military drills in the next suburb, hushed by the distance. The large clock on the wall says seventeen hundred; she has been lying there for a half hour already, but she doesn't mind the wait. She relishes this rare opportunity to slow down; letting all activity drain from her mind more than collecting her thoughts.

She stares at the stained ceiling, savouring her exhaustion. She follows a curious impression she has, that time seems to be expanding and contracting. Is every minute really as long as every other minute, she wonders? If they were different, would she be able to tell? At Minitrue there are occasionally rumours that the management is fiddling with the clocks in the offices to impose longer hours on the workers without telling them. It seems impossible to fool people like that, Julia thinks. She is not fond of conspiracy theories. How could the Party manipulate time to that extent? It is unlikely to work on a practical level, even for the all-powerful Party. The natural time of the day would give them away; when people leave the Ministry and go back out into the outdoors, which they will have to do at some point, the light of day, or lack thereof, would alert them that they have been fooled. And yet something in the deep tiredness she feels in her bones and muscles makes the rumours ring true. It does actually feel as if they were working more hours than before, despite what clocks may say.

A sound of footsteps on the stairs gives Julia a jolt. She is used to having rendezvous with lovers in the dodgiest settings; weirs and moors, abandoned rail exchanges and riverbanks under bridges; more than once she went into the streets during air raids on the city, to take advantage of the confusion for impromptu lovemaking among the rubble. And still this room unsettles her more than any of the open-air locations of her previous love life. Every time she hears steps down the corridor, she fears that it could be the police; every time she pushes open the grimy wooden door, she expects to find someone other than Winston behind it, someone more dangerous than she can handle.

This room was Winston's idea, it was not in the original plans. What is worse, Julia left any mention of it out of her otherwise thorough and accurate weekly reports to O' Brien, and now it is too late to bring it up; mentioning it after the fact would be admitting to having lied. Withdrawing information is a most dangerous crime in Oceania; as an employee of the Ministry of Truth, Julia is painfully aware of this. Daily engaged in crafting and distributing government-sponsored lies on everything, about the past and the present, the public and the private, people at Minitrue know all too well how severely individual initiative in truthmaking is punished in Oceania. Entrusted with the delicate task of producing and manipulating truth, they are bound to even stricter standards than average Party members. As institutional creators of lies, their lying to the authorities will not be tolerated.

So why did she do it? Why did she avoid telling the Party about the rented room? She doesn't really know. Was it to protect Red Face? Is she covering up for him? Is she seeing him as a fellow human being, rather than just a target that was imposed on her by the Party? Or is this an act of rebellion against the Pilot Project E-999 assignment, against the fact that she is kept in the blind about its purpose, against the notion that by tasking her with it the Party has infiltrated the last part of her life that felt as though it was just hers, her sex adventures? She knows that to rebel would be both crazy and unnecessary. Her sex life is still hers, just as much as her sex life has never been hers; sleeping with Party members has always been a way to obtain material benefits, and secure impunity, more than a pleasure in itself. And the impact on her

life, on her time, of this assignment is not that significant in concrete terms. She still can see her other
lovers; she just added a new one to the schedule. Exit
O' Brien, enter Smith.

So why did I do it? It was the reporting; it was the
requirement to submit regular reports that got at me,
made my blood boil in a way it normally never does.
It was not to protect Smith, nor was it to rebel against
O' Brien. It could not help but try to protect my
secrets, my ability to keep secrets in a world of telescreens and thought police. When everyone thought
it was impossible to hide from the eyes of Big Brother,
I had succeeded in doing just that. Because sex was
forbidden, it gained me secure cover. Party members, even Inner Party members, proles, you name it:
they would all get in serious trouble if they were
caught having sex with me, so I could count on their
discretion; they even helped me find places free of
telescreens and hidden mikes. Once I started looking,
there were plenty of places that escaped the gaze of
the Party Control Board; that was my space of freedom, a life that didn't make it into my official record.
Having to report on a sex affair ruined it all. It felt
as if the Party were defacing my work of art, my pre-
cious creature. So I lied to get back at them; if I cannot
refuse the assignment, at least I can still cheat. Like I
have always done, pretend to do as I'm told and then
bend the rules just a little. And yet this feels much
more dangerous than anything I have done so far.

Once again Julia's worries are misplaced, and it is
Winston who appears on the doorstep, with his usual

look of a lamb about to be slaughtered. A wave of relief washes over her. It is a glum kind of reprieve, a lighter nervousness replacing a bigger dread. She is not exactly happy to see him, but at least she is not scared. He is not her supervisor, he is not an Inner Party member; he is just another terrified human being. It is a strange kind of tenderness she feels for this man; not like the warm feeling that pervades her when she sees Jim—who never took up her offer to sneak into the rented room with her, and she never dared mention it again. Not that she has many chances to see him lately; between work and project E-999, she has little chance to hang out at prole bars, or do anything else. All she is left with is this bittersweet nervous affection for her target. As if on cue, Winston rushes towards the bed and embraces Julia clumsily as she sits up, almost ripping her overalls as he pulls at the zipper.

"Oy, careful! I only get one new uniform every five years, like everyone else, darling, and you know how hard to get by are thread and needles these days!"

"I'm so sorry, I…"

Julia laughs in his flushed face, and finishes unzipping herself, kicking her pants off. Winston climbs on the bed, unzipping his own uniforms as she helps him out of it. He moves on top of her, breathing heavily; a pool of sweat forms between their bellies as his body thrusts against hers, in and out, in and out.

Sex with Winston is never great; he is hurried and awkward, moves too much or too little; his hipbones clash against Julia's, his hands squeeze her too hard and in the wrong places. It always feels slightly out of sync; it is not exactly painful, but not exciting either. The bed, on the other hand, is fantastic. The mattress cover is worn in places, the springs have lost their bounciness, and it sags in the centre, but still it feels wonderfully soft and spacious compared to the crammed little cot Julia sleeps on at home, not to speak of the hard and rough surfaces that are usually her outdoor love nests. Like almost every time they have come to this room, after having sex Julia and Winston fall asleep next to each other, naked over the blankets, sweat cooling off in the summer breeze.

When Julia opens her eyes, the large wall clock says eight hundred; like almost every time they have come to this room, she is surprised at how long they have slept. Rather than feeling refreshed, Julia's body feels heavy, her head slow. She lies quietly, watching the man sleeping next to her. His mouth is slightly open; a thin thread of drool shines on his lower lip, and a dark patch is spreading on the sheet underneath it. He has bad teeth, like everyone else in Oceania. Be it bad genes or poor nutrition, we don't seem to be made of very good material these days. The thought makes Julia smile; there is something endearing in this man's tainted body, the way his bad hair, his bad skin, his bad teeth mark him so clearly as a Party member, raised on thin porridge and spongy processed meat, coping with life with large doses of Victory gin and Victory tobacco. As she thinks this, she begins to dimly remember her dream; there was food in it, food the likes of which she had never seen before. Yes, a banquet of some kind, and she and Winston were standing together in front of a laden table, in matching silvery shorts and t-shirts. Or was it a dress? And why is she always wearing silver in her dreams? Was it actually silver? Some shiny material, anyway, very different from their usual overalls, and yet, in the dream, it felt like a perfectly normal outfit for the occasion.

What she remembers distinctly is the food; so many different kinds of it and all so strange. Were there other people with them? All that food could not have been just for them. It must have been some kind of party. There were jars full of brightly coloured confectionery, some in the shape of bears, some in the shape of snakes, some in the shape of tiny white and pink bottles. A plate was covered in tiny ring-shaped candy in pale colours, pastel pink, blue, and yellow, strung on little elastic cords. There must have been other people, after all, because Julia knew that those were necklaces and bracelets, and that you were supposed to hang them on your neck and wrists and crack the candy open from it with your teeth to free it from the cords. Scattered around the table were small yellow plastic bags decorated with bright red rhomboids and lettering of a paler yellow. Some had been roughly opened, revealing orangey bullet-like objects that smelled of cheese. Julia popped one in her mouth and her brain was hit by a sudden wave of pleasure, a mixture of salt, fat, and pure delight.

A large ice box was full of ten-centimetre long parcels, enfolded in shiny paper and plastic. Julia unwrapped one to find inside it, to her horror, a human foot, its pink flesh cold from refrigeration, the toes covered in a thin brown layer. Mould? The colour didn't seem right. What was it, then? A flat wooden stick, similar to a doctor's tongue probe, was attached at the base of the foot. Holding the foot carefully by its wooden handle, Julia sniffed the brown substance, and something immediately clicked. Chocolate! She turned to her companion to share her exciting discovery and found him trying to suck on a piece of bright orange ice from a long and thin paper cone, his face, hands, and arms covered in sticky syrup of the same colour. That also seemed to have come from the box. Looking around, she saw that there were indeed other people, walking around and chatting, absent-mindedly picking candy and ice cream and throwing the coloured wrappings on the lawn. Julia and Winston dug in, their taste buds sing-ing and their bodies floating on a cavalcade of rain-bows.

FOURTEEN.

Back in her dorm, Julia is hard at work typing on the old typewriter in the Common Room. Her bi-monthly report for the ministry's Planning and Development System is due, like every month, by six AM on Monday. Every time I cannot help thinking, why do we have to do a bi-monthly report every month? But of course, questioning the logic of the system will not make writing the report any faster. After being put on project E-999 and having her ration card renewed through a fast track, Julia had briefly hoped there would be an exemption from this too, but of course, no such luck. Better get down to it.

Ministry of Truth, Fiction Department, Technical Division
Planning and Development System
Bi-Monthly Report
July 1984

Julia Unwhite, full-time continuing staff member, Level B Step 4
Staff ID no. 27121975

Part A: Outcomes Sheet

The "Outcomes" sheet is to be completed and returned to the Human Resources Management Service Centre of Minitrue at least 3 weeks before the "Review Date" as notified by the Service Centre of the Ministry. The data on the "Outcomes" sheet will be recorded in the HRM System and a copy will be placed on the staff member's Personnel file. The staff member and Supervisor may keep a copy. Supervisor's copy must be stored securely.

Please answer the following questions to the best of your knowledge. Remember that making a false statement on an official document for the Ministry of Truth constitutes a crime under Oceanian Law.

A1. Key Performance Objective 1: Aligning my professional goals with the strategic goals of the department and of the Ministry.
In the months since my last CPD (June-July 1984) I planned my performance consistently with the Professional Qualities and Strategic Aims of Minitrue, and aligned my goals with those of FicDep, to promote the development and maintenance of a positive, productive and harmonious work environment. Taking a whole-of-Ministry approach, I endeavoured to develop mutual trust, respect, and understanding with my colleagues and my supervisors and enhanced

collaboration with other departments.

A1.2 Timeframe:
June 1ˢᵗ-July 30ᵗʰ, 1984

A1.3 Connecting Objectives and Outcomes
A1.3.1 Which KPAs does the objective relate to?
The objective relates to Key Performance Area no. 2: Creating a harmonious working environment.

A1.3.2 What are the outcomes/benefits of the designated objective?
The outcome of the designated objective is a higher level of coordination within the department and between departments, resulting in a whole-of-Ministry productivity increase.

A1.3.3 Explain how well you met the objectives you set last year, using Key Performance Indicators or measures.
I performed the task to the highest standards as demonstrated by a 100% mark in KPI 5 ("Comrade Peer Evaluation"), indicating high levels of satisfaction with my work. In addition, I improved my working methods based on comrade feedback during meetings (KPI 4, "Oral Feedback at Meetings").

A2. Key Performance Objective 2: Safeguarding Oceania
In the months of June and July, my machine alone produced more than one thousand popular novels for Victory Press, a twenty percent increase on the average production for the same time period in the

previous year. This exceeded by five points the 15% increase goal set by the Ministry. Through increased production of popular fiction for distribution among the proles, my work provided a significant contribution to the social and economic stability of Oceania, our region, and the world.

A2.2 Timeframe:
June 1ˢᵗ-July 30ᵗʰ, 1984

A2.3 Connecting Objectives and Outcomes
A2.3.1 Which KPAs does the objective relate to?
The objective relates to Key Performance Area no. 3: Stabilizing Oceania: protecting our inner borders.

A2.3.2 What are the outcomes/benefits of the designated objective?
The outcome of the designated objective is a higher level of production within the department, resulting in an increase in the production of the department and a whole-of-Ministry productivity increase. A related benefit is the increased social stability due to higher level of popular satisfaction induced by the higher consumption of popular fiction.

A2.3.3 Explain how well you met the objectives you set last year, using Key Performance Indicators or measures.
I performed the task to the highest standards as demonstrated by a 100% mark in KPI 3 ("Productivity"), indicating high levels of satisfaction with my work. In addition, I was selected to represent FicDep at the annual Minitrue Staff Performance Day. I demon-

strated leadership in service by setting an example that induced colleagues to raise their levels of productivity as well (KPI 2, "Leadership and Management").

A3. Key Performance Objective 3: Connecting to the Oceanian Community.

Besides my work in the Fiction Department, in the past three years I have been an active member of the Junior Anti-Sex League, an organisation recognised by the government of Oceania's latest institutional report as one of the top five non-governmental institutions presently active in our region.

A3.1 Timeframe:

January 1978-present.

A3.2 Connecting Objectives and Outcomes

A3.2.1 Which KPAs does the objective relate to?

The objective relates to Key Performance Area no. 5: engagement with the larger community.

A3.2.2 What are the outcomes/benefits of the designated objective?

The outcome of the designated objective is a whole-of-party higher level of productivity, as a result of the conversion from unproductive to productive activities among members. A related benefit is the increased social stability due to lower level of sexual activity among Party members.

A3.2.3 Explain how well you met the objectives you set last year, using Key Performance Indicators or meas-

ures.

Since joining JASL in 1978, I have successfully recruited five hundred new members and I have participated in more than a hundred public demonstrations (KPI 1: Increasing Membership). My dedication to the organisation has been recognised by several prizes, including the prestigious Scarlet Sash, which I received in July 1983 in recognition of my outstanding contribution to the League.

***

Ministry of Truth, Human Resources Department, Personnel Office

Re: Career Planning and Development Report, Julia Unwhite, Full-time continuing staff member, Level B Step 4, Staff ID no. 27121975

Comrade Unwhite,

Regarding your document of July 30th, please be informed of the following:

A1.3: KPA 4, "Oral Feedback at Meetings" has been renamed "Continuous Assessment: Feedback at Meetings" under the New Guidelines. Please amend. You can refer to the Amended Guidelines for the Compilation of CPD Reports issued by the Ministry on April 2, 1984, for further detail.

A.3.3: outcomes of objectives must be expressed in measurable entities. "Several" is not an acceptable description. Please amend.

Part A3: the right margin for this page exceeds the designated limit of one inch. Please amend.

In Solidarity,

Flanagan O' Shanagan
Head of Personnel Office, Human Resources Department,
Ministry of Truth.

FIFTEEN.

It is four hundred and Julia is wide awake; after rewriting the report for the third time last night, she almost finished a bottle of Victory gin, and now her head feels as though it's going to explode. She snuggles back under the covers and tries to go back to sleep, without success. Too many afternoon naps lately have messed up her night schedule, she muses; it's not the first time she wakes before dawn. She hates waking up while it's still dark; in winter it can't be helped, so at least in the summer she would like to be able to sleep until the sun comes out. But nothing doing, sleep is definitely gone from her body. She pulls the dirty sheet off her sweaty limbs and walks barefoot into the communal lavatory, making her way in the faint glow coming from the telescreens.

Another girl is already under the only shower that has hot water, and she gives her a hostile look before turning back towards the wall, huddling under the lukewarm dribble not to waste a single drop. Julia shrugs and opens the tap at the opposite end of the room; the shock of the freezing spray wakes her up and somewhat diminishes the headache. One of the few good things about this year's sweltering August; it actually feels good to have a cold shower in the morning. The water feels delicious on her swollen arms and feet. She lets it run into her eyes and mouth; the strong taste of chlorine seems to wash away the fumes of alcohol from the night before. She leans against the wall, resting her forehead against the cold tiles, and closes her eyes.

An explosion of laughter behind her makes Julia turn; three girls are giggling uncontrollably at some joke that a man standing next to them is whispering with a mischievous smirk. They are all wearing brightly coloured swimsuits and large sunglasses. It must be a swimming event, because behind them is a large swimming pool, and somebody is shouting orders from loudspeakers over an upbeat tune. But the song is not any of the marches Julia is familiar with; and the orders don't sound like any of the orders that you hear at sports events or military parades. "Let's sway!" the speakers bloat. And indeed, people are swaying to the beat coming from the loudspeakers at the shallow end of the pool, which is so packed with bodies that there is barely any room to swim.

At the deep end of the pool people aren't swimming either, but rather floating around on inflatable objects of fluorescent colours of all sizes and shapes. A girl in a bright pink bikini and matching nail polish, that shows off her deep tan, is yelling at the guy who hit the inflatable rubber palm on her floatie, making her spill half of the drink she is holding. She is pointing angrily at the mess of fruit slices and paper umbrellas in her lap, but the music drowns her words and the guy just stares uncomprehendingly, sitting on the pool edge with his feet in the water. As Julia looks at them, trying to make sense of the situation, she realises he is Winston, in silver spandex briefs. A bikini of the same fabric is hanging from the rusty tap of her shower; slipping it on, she steps into the sunlight and heads towards the pool.

Winston is still sitting in the same spot, looking lost, while the lady in pink bares her perfect white teeth in a big smile to a muscular blonde guy offering her a new drink with even more paper umbrellas on it. Julia heads towards him, but before she reaches the edge of the pool, she feels someone tapping on her shoulder and turns, startled. A man in a navy blue short-sleeved polo shirt and matching shorts, sandals on his feet, is standing there smiling.

"Fancy meeting you here, Comrade Unwhite!"

"C-comrade O' Brien. H-hello."

"I see our common friend is here as well! What a nice little gathering. Shall we go say hello to him?"

"Y-yes, comrade, I was actually on my way to…"

"Not so fast, Comrade, not so fast. We have plenty of time. Let us have a chat first, just the two of us. For old times' sake. Shall I get you a drink?"

Holding Julia firmly by the elbow, O'Brien walks away from the pool, towards a small hexagonal hut with a straw roof, surrounded by people standing and holding glasses. Under the roof is a bar, with beer taps and a large number of bottles of different shapes and colours. Everyone sitting at the bar is in their swimsuits, except for the bartender, who is wearing a short-sleeved shirt with a pattern of palm trees and large flowers.

"What can I get you?" he asks, lowering his sunglasses to stare at Julia and flashing his perfectly aligned, pearl-white teeth.

"Victory gin, please, comrade."

"Say what?"

"The lady will have a Blue Lagoon, thank you. And a Kamikaze for me." O' Brien holds a stool for her to sit on, and he perches himself on the next one.

"Coming right away, sir!" with another dazzling smile, the bartender walks to the other end of the bar, where a girl in a wide-brimmed hat with a conical top is waving frantically at him.

"So, Julia. How are things going with our common friend?"

"They are proceeding according to plan, comrade. It took some time to gain Comrade Smith's trust, but I think it is all fine now. We meet about once per week, and I kept track of our conversations as instructed. He has mentioned some unorthodox ideas, but he never expressed direct criticisms of BB nor did he relay any directly counterrevolutionary thoughts. It's all in my latest report."

"Is all really in the report?"

"It is, Comrade. It is my honour to serve the Party to the best of my ability."

The barman puts two cardboard coasters in front of Julia and O' Brien, and a small bowl in the middle, filled with orangey rhomboids. Julia puts one in her mouth and a salty, fatty, cheesy flavour spreads in her mouth. She lets the little rhomboid melt slightly on her tongue before chewing it, closing her eyes for a moment to let the pleasure sink in more thoroughly. When she reopens them, O' Brien is staring at her with an intensity that almost matches that of Big Brother in the newsreels. She shudders but holds his gaze, the Flat Smile back on her face.

"Comrade Smith expressed unorthodox thoughts on three occasions. The first two were complaints about the quality of provisions in the canteen, and the third time he expressed misgivings about the ultimate usefulness of his work at Minitrue. I reported the date and hour of the events, and the exact words he used."

O' Brien is still staring, his mouth just as still as Julia's, his eyes intense as ever.

The barman puts glasses on their coasters; O' Brien's is filled with a cloudy yellow-green dense liquid, Julia's is bright blue. She sniffs at it carefully, wondering if it is poisoned. But if they wanted to kill me, they could do it anytime, in my sleep or after long days of torture; they have that kind of power, always and anyway. They don't need to poison us to get rid of us. What is the point of being cautious? I may as well have a sip, hell, I may as well order a second one too! The drink has a cloying sweetness that is a little nauseating, but still tastes a thousand times better than Victory gin. A pleasant warmth spreads in Julia's throat and in her chest; the headache is now completely gone. O' Brien sips from his glass, winces, and turns back to her.

"You don't need to be so uptight with me, Julia. Relax! We've known each other for a long time. More than known each other. Am I right?" He smiles and leans in towards her, his eyes softening. "You don't need to lie to me. I am on your side. I really am. I realise it is hard to trust anyone in this world, but you have to believe me. Why do you think I came to see you here, instead of waiting for the next debriefing? I am your friend. Please believe me."

"I do trust you, Michael."

"I am here today as a friend, not as your supervisor. I am not here to question you, I am here to answer your questions. You must have so many."

O' Brien gulps down the rest of his drink and gestures for the barman to bring two more of the same. Julia's glass is still half full; she takes another sip of the blue liquid, and suddenly feels unsteady. She holds her head in her hands, breathing deeply.

"Are you ok?"

She feels something wet and hard under her knees, and realises she is crouching on the floor of the shower room, covered in goose bumps, holding her head in her hands.

"Yes, sorry, just felt dizzy for a sec."

"More like a full minute, it seems! Are you sure you're not sick?"

Hovering over her, the girl seems genuinely concerned; she touches Julia's forehead, tucking her wet hair behind her ears. The calluses on her warm, dry palm feel strangely pleasant on Julia's clammy skin. As Julia raises her face, she finds herself staring right into the girl's coal-dark eyes. What is this girl's name again? I don't remember seeing her before. Is she a new arrival? Why is she being nice? Is she a counter-revolutionary? Is she a Party spy?

"I am fine, comrade. Thank you for your concern."

Julia quickly wraps her dripping, naked body in a rough grey towel and rushes out of the common showers, without looking back.

SIXTEEN.

It's a crisp early autumn morning; Julia walks towards work, at her usual brisk pace. It's not cold enough to wear the Party-issued overcoat, but the first autumn winds go right through her threadbare overalls, making her quicken her pace to try and keep warm. At a crossing, a convoy of trucks carrying war prisoners forces her to stop on the sidewalk for several minutes, as rows and rows of gaunt Eurasian faces roll past, blank eyes over hollow cheeks. As she dutifully scowls at the enemy like all the comrades around her, Julia steals a glance at the sky. It is an incredibly bright blue; it is beautiful. It feels as though she is seeing the sky for the first time; almost like an epiphany. She steals another glance, and then another.

I find myself noticing beauty in the world more these days. Is it because I am happier or because I am more desperately in need of happiness from somewhere, anywhere? Is that why my dreams are so intense? Every night, every morning or afternoon nap,

I fall asleep hoping to get back to that place, the one I have been dreaming of lately. Even when I pass out, even when it is scary, still I long to go back to my dream world. It started with the heath and now it turned into something else, yet it is all connected somehow. It is always different and yet always the same. I wouldn't be able to describe it, and yet I recognize it, every time, somehow, I know it is the same world. Glitter, there always seems to be glitter; and music. That unique beat. Fast but slow, enticing; no matter how hard you try, you can't resist, your hips start swaying, your legs start dancing.

Why are my dreams so vivid these days? It all started since they assigned me to Pilot Project E-999. Is it my mind's way of responding to the stress, to the fear of this new task? Or is it rather the excitement of being part of this secret plan, even if they never tell me much about it? I don't know how I feel about this project; it could be a big career step up, or it could end in total disaster. Are they playing me, or am I playing them? Have I sold my soul to the Party after all? Have I retained an inner soul that they can't reach? And if I have retained a soul, if I am keeping secrets from them, then am I playing with fire?

The convoy is gone, and people start walking again, at a brisker pace than before. The Party might encourage its members to show their hatred of the enemy at every opportunity, but it will not condone delays at work because of it. Julia falls into step with the crowd, rushing towards the gates of Minitrue. At seven hundred on the dot, she is in position at her machine, dancing away as the hot steel pops out volume after volume of prole lit. Despite being assigned to a high-level covert operation, she has not been relieved from her usual duties. At the beginning she was disappointed; she had hoped that more privileges would come with the job, adequate to the risks that she is taking. But now she is glad to have her routine; dull as it may sound, her job on the machine gives her pleasure, as it always has. The speed and concentration that it requires free her from thoughts, put her in an almost contemplative mode. The faster she moves, the calmer she feels. She is good at this; this feels good for her.

That evening, as she waits for Winston in the little room over the antique shop, Julia finds herself gazing at the sky again. It is a different shade of blue now, paler and darker at the same time. This, too, is beautiful, in a more subdued way. Sometimes all that we have left is the sky; and besides blue skies in London are such a rarity. They are to be treasured. Her target is late, once again, but Julia doesn't worry as much as she used to. She still has not told O' Brien about the room, but she is less afraid of what would happen were he to find out. After all, he doesn't seem to care about where they meet and what they do; what he wants are detailed reports of Winston's counter-revolutionary talk, and detailed reports of her dreams. She dutifully provides both. She even told O' Brien about the dream in which he himself appeared and offered to answer her questions. That drew a hint of hilarity, more a snort than a bout of laughter, from the man. She knew better than to ask what was funny.

Things have changed significantly from the time he was her lover. She quickly discovered that being in on O' Brien's secret plan gave her less, not more, power over him. Too much is at stake now; she knows that they would not hesitate to kill her if something went wrong. Sleeping with an Inner Party member was fun; working for him on a classified project is downright terrifying. Yet at the same time, she still holds on to the hope that, if she plays her cards right, this could turn really well for her. Maybe much more than the promised promotion to Level B Step 6. Maybe even a jump to level D, or some managerial role in the Ministry. A big promotion, or death after torture; the options are as polarized as they can be. Either way, O' Brien has more power over her than ever. Is this what being involved with Inner Party politics feels like?

When Winston finally arrives, he is in a good mood. He hugs her, kisses her on the cheek, then on the neck, less awkward than usual, almost seductive. Maybe the blue sky affected him as well. After the sex, he starts talking excitedly.

"I had this amazing dream the other night. I just remembered it, I don't know why it came to mind now. It was so strange and so uplifting. I was sitting by a large outdoor swimming pool, and I was in my swimmers, a silvery swimsuit. But it was not a sports training place, and I was not meant to swim. Nobody was swimming, at least not in the normal sense of the word. People were lounging in the water, or standing in the shallow part of the pool, drinking and talking.

Everyone seemed to be merry, as if it was some kind of celebration, but it was, I don't know how to explain, a real happiness, not the kind that you have to display at official celebrations, you know?"

"It sounds nice. Was I in the dream too?"

"Sorry, no, I don't think so... I do dream of you, petal, of course I do. All the time. I rarely remember my dreams, but I know that I have dreamed of you. You mean so much to me."

It irritates Julia when Winston calls her names like petal, or pebble, or kitten, which he does all the time. He seems to think that using this kind of language is a rebellious act, to be affectionate when we should be comradely, to be emotional when we should be rational. She understands that, to an extent. It's not the cheesiness that bothers her; she can appreciate the charm of cheesy, even if she finds it a lame kind of rebellion. But it's always things dainty and delicate that he chooses for her nicknames; he compares her to small animals, little flowers, tiny sea creatures. Why can't he call her a panther, a sunflower, a dolphin? She is no pebble. She is a rock.

"Was any other girl there?" she teases him.

"No, it was not like that, I mean yes, there were both women and men, but it wasn't sexual, or maybe it was, in a way, I don't know. It was just exhilarating; life as it should be. People were free, and happy, and I felt happy and free too."

"I think I know what you mean. I have had dreams like that too, lately."

"See? Even if you were not in the dream, this is still

something we share."

"Hmm, now don't push your luck" Julia punches him lightly on the shoulder; she is surprised at how bony it is. "Winston, have you been eating? Have you lost even more weight?"

"Oh, I'm fine. That's sweet of you to worry! But really you don't need to be concerned. I've just been so excited. And it has been like this since I met you; it has changed my life, you know?"

"I made you sick with love?" she laughs. The earnestness of his reply takes her by surprise and fills her with uneasiness.

"How can you say that?! Love has done me so much good. You have done me so much good. Before, I didn't have anyone I could talk to, someone with whom I could share my thoughts, my real thoughts. Someone who would listen, who was interested in what goes through my mind. But now that I can talk to you, my ideas are more than just fantasies piling up in my head. And I am more and more confident that there must be more people like us, people who hate the system, that don't buy into its lies. Maybe the resistance brotherhood that they talk about really exists, you know. Or maybe if it doesn't exist yet, it will soon. This is why I can dream of happiness and freedom; this is why in my dreams I am happy and free."

"Oh god, again with the brotherhood!"

"Don't mock me. You know, I think that, deep down, you also hope that the brotherhood exists. If there was a way to rebel against all this, if there really was an underground organization that is fighting the authority of Ingsoc, wouldn't you want to be a part of it?"

"I would, dear, you know I would. I just think you are too naïve. You want this brotherhood to exist so badly that you believe it does exist. But do you have any proof? Have you ever met anyone who was a member of this famous brotherhood?"

"You ask that every time. You know I haven't. But that does not prevent me from believing!"

"And you answer that every time. So there you go, we're even." She laughs and hugs him, but he doesn't return the embrace. When he starts talking about his conspiracy theories, he just can't stop. Which of course I should encourage him to do; he's making my job so much easier. But why can't we be a bit more light-hearted, that's what lovers do, after all if this is something I have to do anyway, why can't I have a little fun while I'm at it? But Julia knows that it is more than a wish to play that makes her try to change the conversation. It is also a fear. What does she fear? That if he says too much, she will have to report on him, and will get him arrested, and it will be all over? That if he says too much, she will not dare report on him, and will get herself arrested, and it will be all over? When you live in constant fear, it's hard to tell one fear from another. So I keep going, and fail to deliver on all fronts.

"You know, I remembered something else about the dream."

Jolted from her dark reflections, Julia perks her ears.

"I was trying to think what it was that made people appear so happy and free, and the thing is, in the dream, too, I didn't know exactly. I couldn't understand, and I wanted to. I was so amazed at all these people, how they could be just dancing around in shiny water, under the sun, without a care in the world. And I thought, maybe this is how life was before the revolution. And maybe this is how life could be again; maybe this dream is a premonition. But if this is a glimpse of the future, how can I bring it about? How can I make this dream come true, and how can I do it sooner rather than later? And that's when it happened. Someone approached me, in the dream. Someone I knew."

"And it wasn't me? Now I am really offended!"

"Julia, why do you turn everything into a joke? This is serious. Listen. It was one of our supervisors at Minitrue. Comrade O' Brien. Do you know which one I'm talking about? I think he is the head of Human Resources. He is Inner Party, anyway, of that I am sure."

"Yeah, I think so... white hair, kind of fat?"

"No, no, that's O' Briar, from Communications... anyway, it doesn't matter if you don't know him, the point is, in my dream, he was there, and approached me, near the pool. He seemed quite friendly, very different from how he is at the Ministry, and he told me, I am here to answer your questions, you must have so many."

"And did you? Ask him questions."

"I wanted to, and I was so glad that I could ask him, so happy and grateful and a little scared. But as I tried to open my mouth, that's when the dream ended, and I woke up. And yet, now I remember that clearly, as I woke up I wasn't disappointed, not quite; it was more of a hopeful feeling, as if those answers were really going to come, sometime, maybe sometime soon."

SEVENTEEN.

All reports are to be made in person now. No written traces. Julia cannot tell whether this means that O' Brien trusts her more or less than before. But somehow it seems to be going smoothly; the disaster she keeps waiting for never happens. Weekly debriefings have turned into daily debriefings; even when she has not seen Winston, she has to report. O' Brien makes her go over memories of previous encounters, probing with questions, scanning the recollections for details she might have missed before. The encounters feel less and less like debriefings and more and more like interrogations.

Julia is starting to think that she was not chosen at random for this task; that it is no coincidence that it is her former lover who has become her supervisor, her interrogator. At first she thought that it had to do with O' Brien's lingering attraction for her, that sooner or later he would ask for a fuck on the side, that he wanted an informant with benefits; but that's not it. Rather, she is beginning to realise, it must have something to do with the little interest she has in the system and its plots. Michael knew what kind of person she is. And it's true; she cares very little about it all, the Party, IngSoc, the war with Eurasia, the alleged conspiracies of the underground brotherhood. Only what affects her directly matters to her; she has no curiosity beyond that. Not only does she refrain from asking questions, as Party members are trained to do; she doesn't have any questions, she doesn't care. And they seem to like that; they seem to like her for that. Because she couldn't care less about the meaning of Pilot Project E-999, her reports are entirely neutral; she is a recorder, an instrument. Winston's ideas, his actions, enter her eyes and ears and come out as words. Like when she is dancing in her steel and silicone novel-making machine, she performs her task mechanically, focusing on the rhythm rather than the content. That's how she can dance so fast, that's how she can inform, apparently, so well.

When she has nothing else to report, she must tell O' Brien her dreams, again in minute detail. She has always been quite good at remembering dreams; narrating them is more tedious than actually difficult. Asking Winston about his dreams is far more challenging. He doesn't seem to think they are important; after that one that he was so excited about, where O' Brien made an appearance, he has not mentioned any more dreams, and when Julia asks him, he just says he doesn't remember and changes topic.

"Did you insist? How many times did you ask him?"

"Yes, I did insist. I asked him twice, while were

chatting after making love, and then another time, a few days later, again while doing small talk after sex. I couldn't do more than this, he would get suspicious."

"I decide what you can or cannot do, comrade. Next time ask him again. Find the right moment. Use your girly charm." O' Brien sniggers, and Julia represses a sigh.

"I will."

"Tell me more about that earlier dream. You said it was a swimming event."

"Yes and no, apparently it was an event at a swimming pool, and everyone was wearing swimmers, but no-one was practicing sports. Instead, they were lounging and laughing, having fun."

"And he thought that was a counterrevolutionary act."

"Something like that. I believe the words he used were 'I thought that maybe it was like this before the revolution.' And he said that this might be a premonition of changes to come."

"I see. Go on."

"The other thing is, it's hard to tell, because he seems to remember so little detail, but it sounded like the same place I dreamed about, twice in fact. The first was the dream in which you appeared, comrade O' Brien. Just like you did in Winston's dream. The second dream was very similar, but shorter; you were not in there, but the location was the same; there was a stand that sold liqueur, like a bar but somehow open-air, with potted plants all around. The spirits that they served were sweet and brightly coloured, and they had names I had never heard before: Mai Tai, White Russian, Midori."

"What makes you think it was the same place? You didn't say that comrade Smith mentioned any bar, or plants, or liqueur."

"I know, he didn't, not even when I asked him to tell me about the dream again a few days later. But he is so abstract, he doesn't talk about details like that, ever. All he talks about are concepts, symbolisms, what he sees as the deep meaning of things. What he retained from the dream was this idea that it represented freedom and joy. He wouldn't describe the colours or the smells. But when he was talking about the swimming pool, it seemed like the same one. The way people were lounging in it, the fact that it was sunny, the laughter. And I remembered one more thing. In my dream, I was at the other end of the pool."

"How so?"

"When I was at the bar, I thought I saw Winston. I wasn't sure because he was a bit far away. He was at the other end of the pool. If he didn't look in the other direction, where I was, if he didn't look there at all for the duration of the dream, then he would not have noticed the bar, or the plants. And neither would he know about the liqueurs. It's not just that he doesn't remember them; he didn't see them, not even in the dream."

"Interesting. Tell me more."

"Well, I always see him in my dreams. We spend a lot of time together, and of course I spend even more time going over our encounters in my reports, and then, he is always present in my dreams. But he also must think about me when we are apart, if only to make plans about meeting again, or to worry that we will get arrested. So I wonder whether I am in his dreams too. Whether we are there together."

"Has he mentioned this?"

"No. In fact, when I asked him, playfully, he said no, I was not there in the dream. He was apologetic about it. He is pretty straightforward with me; I don't think he would be hiding something like that. But then it occurred to me that I might have been there. Only he did not see me. Just like he didn't see the bar at the other end of the pool."

"Interesting."

From O' Brien's sudden silence, Julia knows that the session is over. She will be expected the next day at the same time, with more to report. She is not seeing Winston tonight, so he'd better appear in her dreams, or there will be little to talk about.

EIGHTEEN.

But it is not Winston that appears in Julia's dream that night. The dream begins as usual, with the feeling of being in a strange yet familiar place. This one is neither the heath nor the shiny world of sugary liqueurs and purple lights. People are not dancing or laughing or eating; in fact, there are no people in it at all. The space is completely black, and completely empty. Julia looks around, trying to find her bearings; as she turns on her feet, she sees a faint blue light. She moves towards it, walking slowly to avoid bumping into obstacles. But there are no obstacles; just a black void, and that faint light. The light grows brighter, faster than expected, as if the luminous spot were moving towards her as she walks in its direction. As she gets nearer, Julia sees that the light is coming from a bright blue rectangular object, hovering in mid-air in the black space. She cautiously tries to touch it. Her hands feel heavy, clumsy, as if she were holding something. She wants to look at her hands, but she cannot see them. She feels something under her fingers; again, a strange but familiar feeling. It is like being in the novel making machine; an invisible a console rests under her fingers. Instinctively she presses on it, as she does countless time every day. Invisible buttons bounce slightly under her fingers. As she pushes them, the blue rectangle breaks into a myriad of small squares that spread all around her, and she finds herself in a different space.

This one is a vast, barren landscape of bright, solid colours: blue, red, black, green. There are mountains on the horizon, and a crescent moon hovering above them. Julia soon realizes it is a battlefield; dark green-grey tanks are slowly closing in on her. Everything has a slightly unreal feel; the colours are too bright, the lines too sharp, the movements too neat. As the tanks come nearer, Julia realizes she is on a tank, too; she can see the tip of its gun from where she stands, and she knows, without knowing how she knows it, that the console under her hands is connected to the gun. Again, instinctively, she repeats the familiar sequence of gestures, pressing buttons and feeling them respond. Boom! Boom! Boom! Red and black explosions rise from the advancing tanks, one after the other; as they blast, they disappear entirely, soon to be replaced by identical ones. The more tanks she shoots, the more pop up on the horizon. What is this sorcery? And why is she alone in fighting them? But there is no time to think; not only the tanks are advancing, they start shooting too. Wiiin! Goes a bullet right next to her ear. How can it sound so close, if she is inside the tank? But her body is quicker than her mind; bang! Bang! Bang! More tanks detonate and dissolve. The faster the attacks come, the faster Julia moves; this, too, is like being at work, her body and mind moving in perfect sync with the machine. She is the machine; dancing, shooting, fighting, breathing, playing.

But just as she is getting used to the movement, feeling that uncanny calmness of extreme speed, a bullet whistles right next to her from an unexpected direction. How did she not see it coming? Another one, louder than the first. The motherfuckers are shooting from the sky! Green round objects, like flying saucers, rushing at her. As she looks up towards them, the whole console moves with her. Bang! Bang! The saucers explode mid-air, red and black, and dissolve. But the diversion slowed Julia down, and as she looks back at the green plain, two tanks have gotten dangerously close. She shoots in quick succession, left then right, but it is too late; Julia hears a loud explosion right in front of her, and wakes up, gasping, heart pounding.

Except that she doesn't wake up. Someone is resting a hand on her shoulder, gently pulling her away from the console.

"You all right, mate?"

Julia peels herself off from the machine, tries to turn in the direction of the voice. All is black. Has she been blinded by the explosion?

"Here, let me take them off for you."

Cool fingers touch her cheek, and they remove something from her face. A girl is standing in front of her, holding a pair of heavy goggles, like a small-size deep diver's mask, only the front glass is dark, not transparent. It is the girl from the dorm, the one who helped Julia stand up when she fainted in the shower. Shit, why can't I ever remember names?

"Sheila."

"I'm sorry?"

"I'm Sheila. And you are Julia, right?"

"Yes. Julia Unwhite, Ficdep, Minitrue, Party Member No. 271275."

"Yeah, I know. We met before. You don't remember me?"

"I… I think I do, yes. What… where are we? What is this place?"

Julia looks around. They are not in the dorm, nor anywhere that she recognizes from Oceania. If anything, the place looks more like the stuff of her recent dreams. It is one large room, with low ceilings and no windows, lit by soft electrical lamps that fill the place with eerie shadows. The walls are lined with machines that vaguely resemble the novel-making devices, except that there are no printers attached to them, and the screens, about twice as large, are not covered with text but with colourful images. The drawings are in the same primary colours as the landscape Julia was in before; many of them are similar war scenarios, with tanks and aircrafts, while others look more like labyrinths, with roughly drawn people and animals navigating them. People stand in front of the machines, some alone, some in small groups, the ones on the sides peering into the screen while the one in the centre manoeuvres the control buttons and levers. Some are wearing goggles like the ones Sheila took off of Julia's face, and peer inside those with their hands on a console. The ones who look at the screens seem just as absorbed in the world in front of them as the one plugged into the goggles. Loud noises and coloured lights are all around; the atmosphere is of joyful chaos. No-one pays attention to Julia and Sheila.

"Is it the first time you come here? Where did they send you the other times?"

"The other times?"

"When you fainted, the other day. I thought it must be this, but I wasn't sure. And see, I was not mistaken. You've been to places like these before, right? That time, that's what you were dreaming of? That's why you looked so spacey, in the shower?"

"I guess... I don't know what you mean by places like these..."

"Eh! I don't know what I mean either, to be honest. It's hard to describe, isn't it?"

"It is indeed."

"I have come to think of it this way. What it is, is beautiful."

Sheila has laughter in her voice, but she does not seem to be mocking her. It is a kind, empathetic laughter; she seems genuinely happy. Just like the other day, she seemed genuinely concerned.

"Anyway, it's good to see you here, Julia. I knew you were one of the good ones."

"The good ones?"

"I cannot explain more now, sorry. We don't have much time; we will wake up soon. In fact, the dorm alarm has started ringing, can you hear it? We are already waking up. It's just that in dreams time lasts longer, so even though we have no time, we still have a little time."

Huh? Julia just stares back, not sure what to say.

"Ah, don't worry. You will understand soon enough. But now you need to wake up."

As Julia opens her eyes, she sees Sheila's face right next to hers; she is standing next to the bunk bed, her coal-black eyes shining in the cold morning light. She winks, almost imperceptibly, then turns and briskly walks down to where the other girls are doing stretches and push-ups to the sharp orders of the telescreen. Julia jumps down from the bed and follows her. Sheila. That's what her name was. Is she a spy? Is she a counterrevolutionary? Why was she in the dream? Julia chases all thoughts from her mind and concentrates on her calisthenics, the tiniest smile ruffling the surface of her face. What it is, is beautiful.

NINETEEN.

There is something in the light just before sunset that always makes me uneasy. How the sky seems to turn brighter before getting dark, bluer before getting red. Every time I think, what if today is different? What if the sun does not set this time? What makes us believe that the only variables in a day are the ones based on human choice; whether we go to bed early or stay up late, whether or not we have a cigarette after work, whether we wear a jumper over our shirt. Which I should have done, by the way; the evenings are getting chillier and once again I am freezing in my summer uniform, with just the overalls and a light shirt. Will you ever learn, Julia? But yes, why do we only think of those variables, and rest assured that the sun will always set, the night will last a few hours and then dawn will come again. Me, often, I'm not so sure. I look at the moon rising in the evening sky and wonder, what if a second moon rises after the first one? And a third, and ten more? What will I do then?

But alas, there are more immediate variables to think of today. Sniffling in her too-light clothes, Julia closes the window and pours herself a second glass of Victory Gin. Sitting at the bare wooden table in the dormitory's common kitchen, she reflects that she might need a third one to get to sleep. O' Brien's words keep turning in her head; tomorrow is the day, and she must play her part right. If she doesn't, she might end up straight into the Ministry of Love's torture dungeons. Tomorrow O' Brien is going to approach Winston and invite him to his home; he will drop a hint that this has to do with the conspiracy, the brotherhood that Winston always talks about. If Winston does not tell her about this out of his own accord, she must find a way to coax him into talking about it. If he invites her to join him, she must go along. He will probably tell her; he will want her by his side for something like this. He seems genuinely into her, and she has persuaded him that she, too, is a rebel. More importantly, he would never go to something like this all by himself. He is too much of a coward. For all his talk of rebellion, it's clear to Julia that Winston is in awe of Inner Party members; he would not face one of them alone. He needs a sidekick; a cheerleader. And yet, what if he doesn't tell her? What if she is not able to make him talk? What if he smells the trap and they blame the failure of the operation on her? Yes, this definitely calls for a third glass of Victory Gin.

Warmed by the booze and lost in her thoughts, Julia does not hear the footsteps in the corridor, the front door slamming shut. When she walks to the toilets, tipsily and losing balance, she is startled by the silence in the dorm. Not a single girl in the shower stalls; all toilet doors open, the white bowls gleaming faintly in the dim cubicles. She peers into the common bedroom: the bunk beds are all empty, twenty grey sheets tightly pulled over the mattresses, twenty Party-issued nightgowns neatly folded over the thin pillows. Where did everybody go? A chill runs down Julia's spine, shaking off her drunken warmth, until she remembers that it is Hate Week Debriefing Night. Of course! How could she forget the most boring event of the year?

Even more so than other Party-mandated events, Hate Week Debriefing Nights all resemble each other. Since her early teens, Julia has been bored out of her mind by the endless self-congratulatory speeches about the success of the event, the renewed vows to wipe the Eurasian or Eastasian foe off the face of the earth. And by the monotony of the meeting. Hate Week in itself is a rather cheerful event; the parades, the slogans, the shouting, they are entertaining. Even the prize-giving ceremonies, filled as they may be with tedious speeches, have their interesting side. Waiting to hear the names of the winners, looking at their fake smiles and fake tears as they receive their medals; all of Hate Week is a welcome diversion in Party members' grey lives of hard work, bad meals, and cheap gin.

But HWDN is just the worst ever. It almost feels like a punishment for the fun that preceded it. The uniformity is what makes it so unbearably dreary. The reasons for hating Eurasians or Eastasians are nearly identical; no matter whether the enemy of the year is Mongolian or Mediterranean, they are lazy, cunning, depraved; ardent believers of twisted values, irrationally bent on the destruction of socialism. And the reasons for hating them don't seem to change over time either; year after year after year, whether the enemy is Eurasian or Eastasian, their crimes against humanity remain unchanged, their perversions utterly dull. This year was a bit unusual as the enemy switched right in the middle of Hate Week. As the celebrations were in progress, apparently, negotiations at the highest level were taking place, and from one day to the other Oceania was no longer at war with Eurasia, but its ally against Eastasia. The transition was remarkably seamless; there were even speakers who swapped enemy in mid-speech, starting a sentence about Eurasia's immorality and ending it with a proclamation of Eastasia's wickedness. That was mildly amusing. At those speeches, a few people seemed to notice and shifted uncomfortably in their seats. But it didn't last long; very quickly the cheer of military marches drowned all uneasiness, crowds merrily shouting along.

Of course, the debriefing will not mention that; the fact that Oceania was ever at war with Eurasia has already been erased from history, and the evening will all be about extolling the virtues of our leaders and enumerating the depravities of the Eastasian enemy. So, yes, as boring as they get. No second moon rising

tonight. But better hurry: her absence may be noticed, and these days she must play it extra safe. Julia
wraps her red sash from the Junior Anti-Sex League
tightly over her shirt, as she always does for important occasions, and dashes out the door. A few minutes
later, she is quietly sneaking into one of the back seats
in the local council hall, as a middle-aged woman
with grey hair and thick glasses is introducing the
main speaker for the evening, Comrade Brian O' Ryan,
Executive Director of the Hate Week Operations Division of the Hamptons branch.

"Thank you all for coming, comrades. It's been a
very exciting Hate Week this year. And I want to
say up front that this is thanks to your unrelenting
efforts; you are the heart and soul of this event, and
it's been thrilling to see the remarkable amount of engagement and dedication you all showed."

O' Ryan makes a pause to allow the audience to ap-
plaud, which they promptly do.

"We had more than seventy million participants,
exceeding by 25% our target for 1984..."

Julia's attention tunes out as the man's voice
drones on with more statistics, all of them obviously
made up—does England even have seventy million
people? And of course, the proles never even come to
these events, it's only Party members, and only because they have to.

"But it is crucial, comrades, not to stop at Hate
Week. We should not just go back to our offices and
forget all about it until next year. Remember: the
enemy never rests, and neither should we. This is why

we created a Hate Week Transformation Force, which will develop operational strategies to ensure high hatred retention rates and to maintain our record of outstanding deliverables in externalisation of loathing.

At its first meeting this morning, the HWTF has designed a format to ensure that party members take away from this Debriefing Night, a number of targeted insights and actionable strategies for accelerating this transformation agenda. From now on, in addition to Debriefing Night, the HWTF will hold weekly training sessions, on topics spanning from leading complex transformations to solving key operational challenges, in order to support all party members in operationalising the Transformed Hate Week. HWTF training sessions will be held every Friday night at your local community centre. Attendance is, of course, entirely voluntary."

Meaning, of course, entirely mandatory. Julia sighs; just what she needed, another series of useless evening meetings. And of course, since her participation in O' Brien's operation is entirely secret, she will not be exempt from the training sessions; she will dutifully attend them all, sitting in the first row, like the dedicated and enthusiastic party member she incessantly performs as. She will have to find a way to sneak in some Victory Gin.

"The training sessions will be divided into three categories, based on the key priority areas identified by the HWTF. The first set of sessions will focus on leading transformation, exploring the best practices in leading strategy change and operationalising enemy hate strategy transformation. The second set of sessions will focus on accelerating implementation, devising innovative practical solutions to key operational challenges which may prevent successful implementation. The third set of sessions will focus on one-on-one solutioning, leveraging high-impact, ten-minute solutioning sessions with a senior member of the Weekly Task Force leadership."

The speaker's words become an indistinct mumble as Julia dozes off, her arms falling to her sides, her wrists painfully slamming on the wooden bench. She shifts in her seat, and her hand hits something softer than the bench, something alive, warm; another hand, that holds hers gently but firmly. That known touch; the same dry, slightly callused palm that felt so soothing on her wet cheek in the shower, is now arousing as it is comforting. Julia doesn't dare turn, yet she doesn't need to look to recognize that hand. Slowly, she sits up and stares straight ahead, in the vague direction of the speaker. Heart trembling, all her senses concentrate in that one spot on her palm, where a smooth fingertip is now moving ever so slowly up and down, casually tracing an eight shape, again and again and again. Forget about Victory gin; this takes her mind off the HWTF, O' Brien, Winston, tomorrow, everything.

TWENTY.

After a full day of work, Julia's hangover has not yet faded; head pounding, she winces at Winston as they start walking away from the gates of Minitrue.

"You walk ahead. I'll follow. Don't turn back, I'll make sure I don't lose you."

"Are you ok, Julia? You look so pale."

"I'm nervous; of course I am. We both are. You look terrible too, you know! It's a pretty big deal."

"It is. But it's exciting. This is it, Julia! This is the first day of a new life!"

"Ok, ok, now walk on, pretend we are not together. We don't want to be stopped by the Thought Police before we even get there. Just remember, don't look back, I'll be following, I'll make sure I don't lose you. Now go!"

Winston hurries down the sidewalk, and Julia follows him after a couple of minutes. She does not need, of course, to keep track of him. She has been to O' Brien's place so many times she could walk there blindfolded. The streets are damp after the rain, black and shimmering in the fading light of dusk. Julia tries to focus on the colours and smells, to let the surroundings sink in; the details fill her mind and calm her down. The hangover was a blessing in disguise; it made her surprise at Winston's announcement that O' Brien had invited him to his home appear genuine when he whispered it to her at lunch. He invited her along as a matter of course; there was no need for coaxing. He doesn't suspect a thing; of this much she is sure. And now her pale face gives her the appearance of being jittery about the meeting that is about to happen, adding even more credibility to her role as sidekick, dragged along and carried away by Winston's enthusiasm. Except that in this case, her nervousness is genuine; it is not, like for Winston, the impatience of curiosity and hope, but a darker, deeper tension, that ties her stomach in a hard knot.

A few metres ahead of her, Winston is knocking on a large wooden door; no, he is not knocking, just gently pressing on it. The door is unlocked; it gives way easily under his hand; a wedge of light shines on the wet pavement, and he is gone, swallowed by the rising darkness of the evening. Without looking around—the first thing to do when you think you may be followed is to act as though you don't think you are being followed—Julia reaches the door and pushes it gently.

In the lobby, they are welcomed by a handsome man in his thirties, black-haired and olive-skinned; despite the white jacket and black tie, he does not seem to be one of O' Brien's servants. Or at least, Julia has never seen him before. Is he new? Is this a trap? But it is too late to go back; whoever this man is, he is already taking their coats, welcoming them with a courteous but tight smile. Winston hesitates to give his coat, suddenly panicky, a fish out of water. Taking her cue from his awkwardness, rather than handing her jacket to O' Brien's butler like she did many times before, Julia drops it clumsily to the floor, bumping her head against the man's white sleeve as they both bend to pick it up. After hanging the coats in the cloakroom, the butler leads the couple down a softly lit, carpeted corridor.

Trying to distract herself from the knot in her stomach, Julia looks around, taking in more details than ever before. The house is truly beautiful; it exudes wealth and comfort. The thick carpet makes their steps hushed; the wood-panelled walls reflect the light with a soft shine, giving the whole space a feeling of warmth and cosiness. Small carved wood cabinets against the walls, positioned at regular intervals, hold painted ceramic vases with a few tastefully arranged flowers. Flowers! Were there flowers in the house when she came here before? Was she too edgy to notice them? Did they add them to impress Winston? And where do they grow flowers, when all land is devoted to pasture or agriculture? Inner Party members have access to everything. Even impossible things.

The butler shows Julia and Winston into O' Brien's studio. Sitting at his desk, artfully positioned in the pool of light thrown by a single desk lamp with a green lampshade, O' Brien is looking at some papers, ignoring the newcomers. The telescreen on the wall next to him is reciting the latest figures for iron production, that this month have, for the third time in a row, exceeded the target by 25%. The scene almost draws a sigh of relief from Julia. The knot in her stomach loosens slightly. How many times has she seen O' Brien play this part? Sitting at his desk, with an air of importance, making her wait, just a little longer than she is comfortable with. It all feels so familiar it's almost soothing.

At last O' Brien lifts his eyes from the papers and acknowledges Julia and Winston's presence with a frown. He gets up from the desk and approaches them at a slow, deliberate pace. O' Brien doing O' Brien, Julia thinks. Now he will casually switch off the telescreen, with one flick of the hand, without stopping in his stride or taking his eyes off of us. And sure enough he does; the scene matches Julia's imagination so perfectly that it draws a small gasp from her. But it is Winston who exclaims:

"You can turn it off!"

"I can turn it off." O' Brien replies in a blasé tone, as if he were stating the obvious. So this performance is not just to impress girls, thinks Julia.

"Are you going to say it, or shall I?" O' Brien's intense gaze is directed exclusively at Winston, completely ignoring her. Trying to gauge what is expected of her, Julia eases into her role as a spectator of the two men's dialogue, acting surprised and impressed.

"I will say it. We are here because we think that there is a conspiracy against the regime, and we want to join it."

Winston looks warily behind his shoulder; the butler has come back with a black lacquered tray holding a crystal decanter filled with a dark red liquid and three crystal glasses.

"Don't worry about Martin. You can say anything in front of him; he is deaf. That's why I hire him to serve on special occasions like this one."

Martin? A deaf butler? Ok, this was definitely not one of the house servants when I came here before. I guess those were not special occasions, hey?

Martin rests the tray on a low table, pours the garnet-coloured liqueur and serves them one glass each. The thin, chiselled crystal goblet is light in Julia's hand, and gives the liquid inside a dusky glow. Despite the tense situation, holding the glass is thrilling. She has never tasted wine before.

"Is this... wine?" Winston is beside himself. "I had heard about it, but I've never seen the real thing... it smells... amazing..."

This draws a little smile from O' Brien; a benevolent look softens his eyes for a moment. This shift, too, Julia has seen before. It was the core of their courtship, before Pilot Project E-999, before amorous encounters turned into weekly debriefings and weekly debriefings turned into daily interrogations; that moment when the frown turned into a smile, that softening of the eyes, there was something about it that inevitably caught her off-guard. And now it seems to have the same effect on Winston.

"You are correct, comrade Smith. The Brotherhood does exist. But it is not easy to become a part of it. The Brotherhood expects absolute devotion to its cause."

"We are absolutely devoted to it. We are."

"Are you prepared to do anything that could be required of you?" O' Brien's piercing eyes seem to want to hypnotize the younger man. Julia moves closer to her lover and slides her arm under his. She feels Winston relax slightly under her touch; she seems to catch a glimpse of approval on O' Brien's face.

"Yes."

"Are you prepared to die?"

"Yes."

"Are you prepared to kill?"

"Yes."

O' Brien's list of demands goes on and on; to each question, Winston promises with renewed enthusiasm to perform hypothetical illegal and immoral actions in the name of the Brotherhood. All along Julia stands next to him, calming him with her touch and implicating herself with her silence. This may be why she is here; leading Winston into his trap was not enough, she must stay by his side within that very trap, to soothe him and prod him through the process, or the project will not work, it will be all for nothing. She seems to have played her part well enough, because after toasting with the young couple to their joint initiation into the Brotherhood, O' Brien signals to Julia that she is dismissed. He needs to talk to Winston one-on-one now; her presence is no longer required. A flicker of white in the corner of her eye; Martin is already opening the door for her. It took no more than twenty minutes, and all in all, it went more smoothly than she had anticipated. O' Brien's face as Julia leaves is still as impenetrable as usual, but she cannot help feeling, together with relief, a glimmer of hope. She might, after all, get that promotion.

As she walks down the corridor, the sound of her steps hushed by the thickly woven carpet, Julia hears O' Brien ask from behind the closed door of his study: "And I assume you have a hiding place?" A chill runs down her spine as she hears Winston's petulant voice, and knows, without hearing the words, that he is giving him the address of the room above the antique store. The room where they spent many an afternoon over the summer, on that soft, wonderfully comfortable old bed. The one not-so-trivial detail that she had left out of her reports.

TWENTY-ONE.

Wrapped in Jim's arms, Julia breathes in the mix of engine oil and tobacco that clings to his clothes. After several weeks apart, their lovemaking has been urgent, hungry. Clothes still on, they pulled at each other's hair, twisting their heads at painful angles, holding so tight they left red marks on each other's skin. They went on and on, from behind, facing each other, lying down, standing. He slapped her buttocks, hard, as he mounted him, and urged him to move faster and faster. "You like that, don't you? You prole slut!" she laughed, "I bet you want..." her words turned into moans as he rubbed her breasts, sending warms shivers through her body. Julia had missed the wildness and the abandonment; it's so different than it is with Winston. Proles do it better, no question about that.

"I gotta go, Jimmy."

"Already, princess? What's the hurry? I thought they had let you out early today. Trying to exceed your monthly quota of trashy novelettes again?"

"Yeah, you know what a dedicated comrade I am! No, but I have something to do. It's kind of work related, but it's not at Minitrue."

"So mysterious! My lady of enigmas. You sure you're not a secret agent or something?"

"I'm sorry, Jimmy. I wish I could stay longer, I really do. To be honest, right now I would give anything to stay here with you, rather than go where I have to go."

"Oh come on, it can't be that bad, can it? Look at it this way. Whatever it is that you have to do now, tonight you'll have a glass or three of your Party members-only disgusting booze and you will forget all about it."

"Maybe. Or maybe not."

Startled by her tone, Jim props himself up on an elbow and looks into Julia's eyes. "Babe, are you ok? I've never seen you like this. You're really pale."

"Yeah, I'm ok, thank you, Jimmy. I'll be fine. Just… if…"

"What is it?"

"If you don't see me again, it won't be because I stopped liking you. It won't be because I decided to dump you. I want you to know that. Please believe me."

"Jules, Jesus, what are you talking about? Now you're scaring me."

"Nothing. Sorry, I am just feeling sentimental, I think I'm still hangover. Maybe you're right about Party member booze. It makes me sick for days. I should drink less."

"Whatever you say, babe."

"It was great to see you. I had missed you. A lot."

"Well don't wait so long to come back next time. Don't want to make this handsomeness go wasted, hey?" Jim laughs and kisses Julia all over the face, the ears, the neck, until she giggles and wriggles herself free.

"Bye, Jimmy. Take care."

"You too, missy."

With a heavy heart and heavier feet, Julia walks over to the room above the shop. Winston insisted on meeting there after work, and she couldn't say no without arousing suspicions. The fact that Winston is still running free, that they did not arrest him right after she left O' Brien's house, is mildly encouraging. They probably want to observe him further; and they want her to continue in her role, as if nothing happened. But this is just a guess; what exactly she is expected to do, she is not sure. Not a word, alas, from O' Brien. Not that she expected anything different. Being useful to Inner Party members does not make you one of them. She has never been privy to their intentions and she never will be; when no instructions are coming, she is supposed to improvise, but if she makes a mistake, the responsibility is all hers. What a nice position to be in.

Winston is already waiting for her in the room; he looks more excited than she has ever seen him. No sign of O' Brien or the police, thank god. Just a shiny-eyed Winston, pacing around the room with a big smile on his face.

"Look what he gave me!" without even greeting her, let alone hugging or kissing her, Winston thrusts a leather-bound volume into Julia's hands.

"A book?"

"The book. Immanuel Goldstein's book."

"Immanuel Goldstein's book about what?"

"Everything! It explains it all, Julia. The regime, how they set it up, how they are tricking us, how they are faking news and historical records, all of it!"

"But we already knew that… we both work for the Ministry of Truth, Winston. We of all people should know that news and historical records in Oceania are manufactured by the Party."

"No, you don't get it, darling. It's much more than that! It's all here, in the book. That's why I brought it, I want to read it to you, to explain it to you." Winston's visible irritation at Julia's lack of enthusiasm does not lessen his own fervour. Without waiting for her response, he takes the volume back from her hands and sits on the bed, leans his back against the wall, and opens the heavy tome in his lap. Realising he's not going to change his mind, Julia crawls under the covers next to him, nestling her head under his arm in her best listener pose. She may as well continue playing her role. After all, that's what she has become. The hand that rocks the cradle.

After a few minutes, however, the relief of not having been arrested, the warmth of the blanket, and the flat tone in which Winston reads all combine to make Julia sleepy. The more she tries stay awake, the drowsier she feels. Fighting the urge to sink down into the soft, cozy bed, to keep herself awake she tries to listen more carefully, occasionally interrupting to ask questions.

"See, what the book shows is that we were not crazy after all. This is more than our speculation; it is written proof that the Party is engaging in this constant distortion of truth. All along, my question was, why? Why is life so painful in Oceania, why do we need to be so unhappy all the time? But of course, I get it now, and isn't that obvious? It is what the Party wants, so they can keep us down, make us forget that there ever was a better life, that there could ever be a better life. This book is explosive, Julia! It really tells it like it is. The facts are all there."

"What facts?"

"How the Party gained its power by halting progress and diminishing wealth. Its main goal is to make us poor and unhappy. It makes so much sense when you read it. See, it explains it so well: 'In a world in which everyone worked short hours, had enough to eat, lived in a house with a bathroom and a refrigerator, and possessed a motor-car or even an aeroplane, the most obvious and perhaps the most important form of inequality would already have disappeared.' You understand what that means? We do not live in poverty by chance; it is a conspiracy! They need us to be poor and unhappy so that equality cannot be achieved, so that we will not revolt against them!"

All the hours spent in this room, away from telescreens, seem to have made Julia bolder; or perhaps it is the fact that Winston's enthusiasm is so out of tune with her own feelings of dread. Normally she would keep quiet, but today she can't help voicing her disagreement. And it feels strangely good to do that; sometimes Julia thinks arguing with Winston is way better than having sex with him; or maybe good arguing makes up for the bad sex. Suddenly taken by the topic, she lets herself run with the conversation, forgetting her fears.

"Mhh ok... but aren't people easier to manipulate when they are happy? What's the point of denying people basic things like a home and a bathroom? They will just become restless and when they are restless, that's when they become less easy to control. That's why we make trashy novels for the proles, isn't it? To keep them happy so that they don't rebel?"

"Oh, Julia, sometimes you are so self-centred. The world does not revolve around your novels for the proles, you know? Let me explain it to you. If people had everything they want, they would no longer accept authority as they do now. If everyone had a bathroom and a refrigerator and a motorcar and an aeroplane... imagine having your own aeroplane! Wouldn't that be amazing? And the only thing that stops us from having that is the Party; they deliberately hinder economic and technological progress so that we cannot have these things. But if people had houses with bathrooms and refrigerators and motorcars, then they would start thinking, then they would question the privileges of the ruling class, and revolt against the Party!"

"You just wish you had an aeroplane, Winston."

"Well why not? Wouldn't that be great if everyone had their own private aeroplane?"

"I don't know... where would they put them? Everyone would want their private airport, next to their private house with bathroom and refrigerator, but where is the room for all these houses with carports and air-ports? What about the noise and the fumes from all the cars and the aeroplanes, won't people be miserable in this crowded, noisy, polluted world? And who would pay for all of this, the houses, the motorcars, the aeroplanes? Where would all the money come from?"

"But that's the point, Julia! The money must be there; it's just that they hide it from us, they keep us poor on purpose. But if technological progress resumed at the pace it had before socialism, then people would naturally become smarter, and realise they are being fooled, and they would demand what is theirs. The Party would not be able to hoard all the wealth anymore. And then there would be money for everyone, there would be motorcars for everyone, even aeroplanes for everyone."

"I don't know, Winston. It seems to me that if everyone had refrigerators and motorcars, those things would keep people distracted from the fact that the elite have even bigger houses, fancier motorcars, more powerful aeroplanes. The elite would still hoard the money, and the masses would still not realise it. The houses and cars would be for common people what the novels are for the proles now. Just like they read their trash, we would drive our cars and fill our fridges and redecorate our bathrooms, and forget to look into the bank accounts of Inner Party members."

"Again with the novels for the proles! Julia, sometimes you are so stubborn. Let me read more to you, if you listen carefully I'm sure that you will get it."

As Winston goes on reading, another wave of drowsiness washes over Julia, and she finally closes her eyes. Winston's words turn into a confused dream in which she is rewriting the history of Oceania with the novel-making machines, turning politics into pornography, and adding coloured illustrations of cars, airplanes, and refrigerators with scantily clad busty women and muscular men posing next to them. After a while Winston too begins to come down from his agitated state; sliding further under the blankets, he snuggles up to Julia and closes his eyes. The monotone of the reading is replaced by an equally regular soft snoring sound.

TWENTY-TWO.

Julia wakes up feeling rested and refreshed, as she had not felt in a long time. Yet the clock on the wall says only twenty hundred thirty; considering how long Winston had been reading, she must have slept for thirty minutes, forty-five at most. The perfect nap: short enough not to waste too much time, intense enough to fully recharge you. Winston is standing at the window in his baggy underwear, looking down into the courtyard. A faint grey light fills the room; reflections from the streetlights throw sharp shadows on the faded wallpaper. The clouds are hiding the moon; or maybe it is too early for the moon to have risen, and the clouds are just hiding a dark sky. Julia gets up, covered in goose bumps, and hugs Winston's skinny body from behind, resting her chin on his shoulder. He seems so fragile as he stands there naked; a wave of tenderness sweeps over her at the thought.

"We are the dead," murmurs Winston.

"We are the dead?" Julia frowns, perplexed. What

does he mean?

"You are the dead." A voice booms from behind them. They both turn in shock, still holding hands, shivering.

"It was behind the picture!" cries Julia. How could I be so stupid? I heard Winston give them the address! How could *he* be so stupid? Of course they would put a telescreen in the room; we served it to them on a silver plate.

"It was behind the picture," repeats the voice behind them. "Stay where you are. Put your hands on your head and turn your back against each other. Slowly. Do not make any sharp movements."

Suddenly they are storming in; men in riot gear, with shiny black helmets and shields. Thick black boots stomping the ground, running up the stairs, swarming in from the window. It seems to Julia as though there were hundreds of them, rushing in from all directions, filling the room until it is about to burst. The policemen are only fifteen, but that is more than enough to make escape impossible. Julia feels a sharp pain in her right shoulder and finds herself kneeling on the floor, breathless. A cracking sound, a hot lick on the side of her face, blood filling her field of vision. A bullet? But there was no sound of a firearm; no smell of smoke. Julia's hands instinctively search for a keyboard, buttons to press to fight the invisible bullets closing in on her. But this is no game; there is no keyboard and there are no bullets.

Soon she realises that the cracking sound comes from the policemen's truncheons, crashing against the hard bits of her body, where bones protrude under the skin: her shoulders, her ribcage, her skull. Then softer, squishy sounds, as it hits her face, her abdomen, her thighs. They must be holding the truncheons upside down, using the ribbed handle to hit; she senses this more than seeing it, from the sharpness of the ache. Short, hot flashes of pain explode all over Julia's body; she crouches further, balling up to escape the blows, but there is no escape, they just keep coming on her curled-up body. Eyes on the ground, she tries to listen for O' Brien's or Winston's voices, but her ears are ringing in her throbbing head. Sounds gets softer and more distant, until everything turns black. Folded in two, Julia concentrates on her breathing, trying to stay alive, trying to resist the pain. But it is too much to bear, too much to resist. She feels herself losing grip on reality, a wave of pain and fear washing over her. And then it happens: the ringing in her ears grows both louder and smoother, turns into a familiar sound. The reddish darkness inside her eyelids grows deeper and brighter, turns into a familiar colour.

Waves are crashing on the sand with a loud, monotonous sound; city lights in the distance look like scattered jewels, orange and white and yellow gemstone shards against the black sky. The night air is hot and moist on Julia's bare arms; she can taste salt as she licks the sweat beads that are forming on her upper lip. The hem of her dress sticks to her legs, rough grains of sand cling to her feet as she walks by the shoreline. A few metres from the water, people are crouching around a bonfire, singing; a young man is sitting cross-legged, a guitar in his lap, while others crouch and squat in a rough semicircle. Their shadows flicker in the reddish darkness over the sand. One black silhouette peels itself from the cluster, becomes sharper as it nears the glowing flames, standing, then grows dimmer and larger as it leaves the group, walking towards the water.

"You made it. It's so good to see you, Julia."

"Do I know you?"

"It's me. Come away from the shore, the tide is rising, you're getting your dress wet. Take my hand, let's go where there's a bit more light."

Before they even reach the lampposts that line the ocean road, Julia recognizes the hand that firmly and gently holds hers.

"What am I doing here, Sheila? And what are *you* doing here? What is this place? Who are those people? Is this a dream? What happened to me?"

"Always so many questions! You managed to come back here, sweetheart. That's the most important part."

The singing in the distance is interrupted by scattered bursts of laughter, then recommences, louder. The tempo is more upbeat, and drumming joins the notes of the guitar. It has a ringing sound, as if it were coming from a tin barrel. The orange light of the lamppost makes the sweat on Sheila's collarbone shine; a drop trickles down the neckline of her tank top, nestles between her breasts. She wipes a strand of wet hair from her neck with her left hand, still holding Julia's wrist with the right. A gust of ocean breeze blows on the two women's flushed faces, and they quickly close their eyes in unison, their faces almost touching. Her eyelids shut tight, all Julia wants is to lose herself in this moment. Throw your arms around me. Hold me tight and keep me here. Please.

Feeling a squeeze on her shoulder, she opens her eyes again.

"This won't last long, Julia, so listen carefully. You will wake up soon. They came to the dorm today, to search your bed and your belongings; they asked us all sorts of questions. This can only mean one thing: you got caught. I don't know what you were doing, but whatever that was, this is the end. You won't be put back on the project, and neither will you return to your job at Minitrue. Your old life is over, mate. They will take you to Miniluv, and we both know what they do to people there. But you don't need to be afraid. You can come back here. You found your way once, so you know how to do it. You just have to remember the way; find it and follow it. They don't control everything, Julia. That's why there is hope. I will be waiting for you. Now go. Wake up."

TWENTY-THREE.

Julia wakes up feeling battered and bewildered, more than she has felt in a long time. Bandages partly cover her face, and her wrists are strapped to a bed's metal railings—she can feel the cold bars against her skin, the tight leashes digging into her flesh. From a fissure between the bandages her eyes can vaguely make out a brightly lit room. Everything seems to be white: the ceiling, the walls, the floor, the beds, the bedsheets, the inmates' gowns. Is this a hospital or a prison? Is she a prisoner or a patient? Of course, she is both; although she has never seen pictures of this place before, Julia has no trouble recognizing it. She is in the Ministry of Love.

"Good guess, Comrade Unwhite. That's exactly where you are."

Julia tries to turn her head in the direction of the voice, and a flash of pain shoots through her neck. Is her head held in place by straps too? Or is it just the pressure of the bandages on her bruises? But she cannot see anyone else in the room; just lines of inmates in white gowns, lying motionless under their white sheets, strapped to the beds' metal railings. Everything is shiny and quiet; the only sounds are the faint hum of the neon lights and the soft whirring of engines powering the intravenous drips attached to each inmate's bed. So where did this voice come from? Could it be just in her head?

"Good guess, Comrade Unwhite. That's exactly where I am."

Is that O' Brien? The voice sounds somehow deeper, huskier, as if it belonged to an older man; but there is a certain similarity, as if this was a version of O' Brien. Is that how voices sound inside our head?

"You have disappointed us, Comrade. You betrayed the trust the Party put in you."

As if you ever had any trust in me. Or anyone for that matter. A sarcastic snicker turns into a gurgling sound in Julia's swollen and sore throat. Even uttering such a soft chortle is so painful that it leaves her breathless for a few seconds. She remembers reading somewhere that post-surgical pain makes your breathing shallow, and that can give you pneumonia. She tries to make her breaths deeper; tries to relax her tensed muscles and ease into the pain, to help her body heal. She needs, first of all, to keep herself alive.

"The Party does not look kindly upon traitors, Comrade Unwhite. You were entrusted with a particularly sensitive task, working on a project that the Party has invested valuable resources in. Failure to achieve your goals would have been bad enough; but you withheld information from the Party. To do so is inexcusable; this kind of betrayal will not be tolerated. The punishment will be proportionate to the crime."

Of course, I knew all along that I was playing with fire; I knew getting caught was a distinct possibility. And yet somehow I never stopped to think about what would happen afterwards; and now here I am, facing the unexpected. How bad can it get? Curiosity mingles with fear in Julia's confused head. The dull pain all over her body reminds her of what she survived. It was terrible, yes, but here she is, on the other side of a brutal beating, conversing with O' Brien in her head.

"How bad can it get, you ask? Your curiosity will be soon satisfied, Comrade, don't worry."

The voice now sounds different; somewhat metallic, as if it were coming from a machine. Is there a telescreen somewhere in here? Julia squeezes her swollen eyes, trying to make out the details of the device next to her bed. It looks like an ordinary intravenous drip. A soft plastic pocket filled with a transparent fluid is hanging from a metal railing; behind it rests a dark monitor striped with glowing green lines. Is that where the voice comes from? But it looks nothing like a telescreen; more like ordinary hospital equipment. She cannot lift her head enough to look at her arm but wriggling it slightly she can feel something hard pressing against it; probably a cannula inserted in a vein. Except for the straps that she feels on her wrists, the bed equipment looks and feels exactly like the one in which she spent her recovery days when she had an appendectomy as a teenager. So where does the voice come from, if not from the machine? Is her mind playing tricks on her? And how can there be no telescreens in a London building?

"We can make the physical pain stop, you know. Oh, don't look so scared. I am not talking about killing you. Not yet. Look again at the IV drip next to you, comrade. See there is a second, smaller drip bag behind the first one? That is filled with a powerful painkiller. We can connect it to the saline solution bag and send the painkiller directly into your bloodstream. Would you like us to do that?"

Julia gasps, and pain reverberates through her ribcage. She tries to steady her breathing. Is this a trick?

"So mistrustful, Comrade Unwhite. Typical of traitors. You all think that because you are untrustworthy, others must be too. Have a little faith, Comrade. We want, after all, to keep you alive. If we wanted to kill you, we could have done so long ago."

Julia closes her eyes, trying to gather her thoughts. Is this voice even real? How can she hear it in her head? And more importantly, how can this disembodied voice listen to her thoughts, when she is not putting them into words? Is it gauging her reaction from her facial expressions? Is she talking without noticing it? Be that as it may, she must admit that the voice is right. Whoever is keeping her here must, for some perverse reason, want to keep her alive, at least for a little longer, or she would be dead already. Well, she wants to stay alive too. Pain equals shallow breathing equals pneumonia. Pain equals fuzzy mind equals less of a chance to make it out of here.

"Yes," she whispers. Her voice sounds so hoarse she almost doesn't recognize it.

"What is that, comrade?"

"Yes, I-I... would like... t-the... painkiller. P-p-please."

"There, you see? It wasn't that hard to say yes, was it?"

Relief floods Julia's mind as her body is released from pain. Can it be this instantaneous? The absence of pain is almost pleasure. Breathing freely feels utterly delicious. A drowsiness comes over her, sweet and warm, and O' Brien's voice suddenly sounds gentler, almost tender. Like the softness that sometimes she could glimpse in his eyes, back when he was her lover, a lifetime ago.

"Did you ever ask yourself why this is called the Ministry of Love, Comrade Unwhite? The Party doesn't want to hurt you, you know. You are hurting yourself. Look around you. All these people in their beds, they are here because they have been hurting themselves, with their lies, with their secrets. The more you keep secrets from the Party, comrade, the more you resist, the more you hurt yourself. We want you to stop hurting, comrade. You see, the purpose of this Ministry is not to harm; it is to help. We brought you here so that we can help you embrace your true self, so that you learn to become one with the Party, to love it and be loved by it."

TWENTY-FOUR.

How much time have I spent in here? My wounds and bruises seem to be healing fast; they have removed the bandages from my face, and I can get up from the cot almost without difficulty. Counting from the meals they have given me, assuming there are three a day, I have been in this cubicle for two days and two nights. But when did they move me from the hospital bed? My memories are so confused. Try to think straight, Julia. You can only count on yourself here. Or anywhere. The light is very bright, even brighter than in the communal hospital room. The smells are different too; somehow mouldy, despite the shiny, aseptic look of all surfaces. Am I in a different wing of the building? How far am I from that other room? How big is Miniluv? They must have transported me while I was drugged. Maybe I should not have let them put me on those painkillers; everything has been a blur since I had them. Not that I had a choice. They took me off the drip, but I still feel sluggish. How long until the effect wanes? Or are they injecting me with them still, while I sleep? Would I notice if they did? Is it worse to notice or not to notice? Am I more afraid of knowing or not knowing?

A clanging sound startles Julia, jolting her from her thoughts. A small white flap on the white steel door to her cell opens sharply, and a white tin tray slides onto the floor. Eagerly she crouches down to inspect it. It is divided into four sections of uneven sizes; on the first three, grey-white lumpy gruel, pink-grey boiled meat, and green-grey mashed peas are piled in neat small pyramids. The fourth has a white tin cup filled with water. She sniffs at the water carefully, trying to gauge whether there is something dissolved in it. But all she can smell is chlorine; and besides, what would she do if she smelled something suspicious? She has no access to any other water, and drink she must, or she will not last very long. The food, too, doesn't smell any different from what she always had at the canteen in Minitrue. Apart from the round tin cup, there are no utensils. Julia scoops up the mush with her fingertips; it is cold, and so lean her hands do not even get greasy. After each mouthful, Julia licks her fingers one by one, not to waste a single calorie.

She finishes all too soon; how long till the next meal? And what will she do in the meantime? There are no visible telescreens in the cubicles. Scanning the room, Julia noticed four small round objects in the corners of the ceiling. They must be closed-circuit cameras; she has read about them somewhere. Unlike ordinary telescreens, these have only a receiving function; they do not transmit any image. The place is eerily quiet. At first Julia was relieved to be spared the endless bulletins on the Party's war victories and industrial successes, the hollering of morning calisthenics announcers and the monotone of documentaries about Big Brother's heroic childhood. But soon the silence grew uncomfortable. Without windows or clocks or anything else to measure time by, she is starting to lose her grip on reality. Sounds and images, no matter how boring, would have filled her mind with something other than her thoughts. Perhaps this is what they want: to drive her crazy. In a way, it is worse than the physical pain. How bad can it get?

And yet even worse than the silence are the cries. They mostly happen at night; if that is the night. With no windows and the lights always on, it is impossible to tell; the night has become the time between the meal with meat and peas and the meal with eggs and milk. And the time of the desperate cries. Some are just wordless wails, almost inhuman, like cows dragged to the slaughterhouse. Some are half-sentences, uttered in gasps by hoarse voices, mixed with sobs. They beg, they apologise, they curse, they threaten, they plead. Some call for their mothers, some for their children, as if any of those people could come and save them. They all seem to be terrified of one thing: Room 101.

What is so scary about Room 101? People's confused cries mention drowning, being chased by ferocious beasts, burning in the fires of hell; how can a single room be filled with such terrors? What is Room 101, and what will I do if they take me there too? Not if, but when, I guess. There is very little chance I will be able to escape it. The thought makes Julia shudder as she crawls back on her cot, leaving the clean tray on the floor. After I eat I always feel sleepy. Maybe they are putting something in the water after all. Or is it in the food? Or perhaps it is just exhaustion, and lack of coffee and gin. Victory gin! You disgusting oily friend! Julia never liked the taste of it, always envied the frothy beers of the proles, yet now she would kill for a sniff of its turpentine-like scent, a drop of its fire in her stomach. It was a way to escape reality, to make it more bearable; now all that is left is sleep.

Pulling her hair over her eyes to find some respite from the brightness, Julia curls under the thin white sheet; soon her breathing becomes slower and more regular, and the tension drains from her face.

TWENTY-FIVE.

The clouds are low in the sky; everything is bathed in a soft grey light. It is not particularly bright, yet Julia cannot stop blinking and squinting, as if she were blinded by something. It is more like a spasm in her face; the urge to squint seems to come from inside her, an involuntary movement, like the beating of the heart. She tries to steady her breath and open her eyes more, but nothing doing; her eyes keep blinking madly. So be it. Between the patches of darkness of her dropping eyelids, she looks around. The place looks familiar. Julia takes a few uncertain steps; the ground is soft under her feet. Squinting harder, she sees white sand, scattered with white and orange small cylinders, about one centimetre long. Julia squats down to the ground and picks one up between two fingers. Its inside is white, stained with brown in the middle. It is wrapped in a thin orange sheet, speckled with yellow, a thin gold rim on one end. The paper looks burnt on the gold side. Julia cautiously sniffs at it; it does indeed smell of burning. It is a familiar, somehow pleasant smell.

"You can bum a cigarette off me if you want, darl, no need to pick up butts from the ground!"

Julia stands up abruptly, and the black patches in her vision multiply; a wave of dizziness overcomes her.

"Butts?"

"Cigarette butts. Are you collecting them or something?"

A middle-aged man in a polo shirt is smirking at her, holding out a red-and-white rectangular parcel, its tin foil top partly ripped off, a rolled cigarette sticking out of the opening. The cigarette is topped with a gold-rimmed orange cylinder just like the ones scattered on the ground. Ready-made cigarettes with gold-rimmed tips. Never seen them before, and yet these, too, feel familiar. Through her blinking eyes Julia looks down at her own legs, her thighs, her torso. She gasps.

"I'm not wearing silver!"

"Looks like you're not, I'm afraid, darl," the man sniggers. "You going to a party or something?"

"I... I know this place... this is..."

"Margate Sands, darl. This is Margate Sands. You ok there?" A note of concern has entered the man's voice.

"I know this place... I have been here before..."

"Very likely, darl. A lot of young people come here. It's a pretty popular destination, especially after they revived the theme park. The new owners gave it a pretty stupid name, but they sure did a good job of renovating the place. All those new rides, me kids love them. Come all the time with their friends. Lots of young folks come from London too. That where you from, darl? Coming from London, are you?"

"Yes, I do come from London. Well, I think. I… I might be lost."

"You lost, love? Where you headed to? You got an address?"

"No, I mean… I *feel* lost… something's not right…" The concerned look on the man's face turns to one of irritation; he looks at his wristwatch, shuffling his feet in his plastic sandals. "Well, darl, why don't you rest a little here, will you? You will feel better in a jiffy. See that bench over there? Let me walk you to it, ok?"

As soon as Julia sits down on the orange plastic seat, the man pats her on the shoulder and hurries away. Julia sits and stares, still blinking furiously. Dark patches fill her vision, and a heaviness tightens her eyelids. This, too, is a familiar feeling. I can't open my eyes, they are open but they are also closed, they constantly try to revert to this closed state. It's as if I need to close my eyes to see better. I've felt this before… many times… but when? Why?

And then, suddenly, it dawns on her: it is a childhood memory. Afternoon naps. After waking up at dawn to go to Junior League training before school, exhausted, she used to fall asleep on her desk at recess, the room still brightly lit by the afternoon sunshine. It was a short, uncomfortable sleep, the sharp edge of the desk biting into her bony ribcage, the bright light in the room trying to wrench her out of her shallow slumber. And that familiar feeling; dreaming of being unable to open her eyes. Long, fitful dreams where nothing happened, just that feeling of wandering around with eyes half closed, a mysterious force that tried to squeeze her eyes shut no matter how much she tried to open them. Until she did open her eyes, and woke up, the sun shining on her sweaty face.

I am dreaming. This is a dream, and I am in it. My body is in a cell in Miniluv, the light from the ceiling shining bright on my eyelids. My mind is dreaming this place, moving around in it. This is it, the place I always come back to, the place of glitter and music. This place is in my dream and I am in it and I know it. The thought amazes Julia; the feeling of empowerment is exhilarating. But what now? What do I do with this knowledge? Empowerment, yes, but power to do what? Think, Julia, think. There was something I had to do. There is something that is waiting for me here. No, it is not something; it is someone. I have to find Sheila.

TWENTY-SIX.

"**S**heila!"

Gasping, Julia sits up straight in her bed. Did she actually scream Sheila's name, or was it just in her head? Leaning back against the bed railing, she tries to steady her breath. As she slowly relaxes, fright turns into exhilaration. What just happened? Closing her eyes, she tries to remember every detail of the dream; the sounds, the feelings. The place she visited was the same one she saw when she passed out from the trouncing; it was daylight this time, but the beach looked and felt just the same. It didn't feel familiar despite its strangeness; it felt familiar because of it. Will Sheila be there again if she is able to dream herself back to it? I cannot be sure, but all I can do is try. That's what she said: you need to find your way back here. What will I do when I find her? She will know; she always seems so confident.

Lying back on the cot, Julia squeezes her eyes shut and tries to go to sleep, but she is too excited to feel any drowsiness. She lies still anyway, reliving in her mind her previous visits to the place of glitter and music. The swimming pool, the dancing, the eating. Sheila was never there at the beginning, or was she? There were always lots of people around her, a confused crowd; could Sheila have been among them, and Julia did not notice her because she was concentrating on other things? She tries hard to recall the full picture of each dream, but only images of Winston and O' Brien emerge sharply from the blur of colours and sensations. Trying to guess the time, Julia listens for noises outside her cubicle, but cannot hear any. The night moans of the other inmates have subsided; it must be morning.

Julia gets up and begins her calisthenics routine; even though there is no telescreen to order her to practice them, she has gone back to them as soon as her fractures healed. You must keep fit to survive. Even if you don't know whether you will make it out of here alive. The day passes very slowly; a tray of eggs, milk, and mushy oatmeal, a tray of mashed potatoes and baked beans, a tray of peas, gruel, and boiled meat. Between meals, she exercises some more, to pass the time and hoping to get tired. Evening brings drowsiness and expectation; pulling her hair over her eyes, Julia rests her head on the hard cot and slides into a restless slumber.

Waking up is a vast disappointment: not only she has not found Sheila, she doesn't seem to have dreamed at all. In that moment of epiphany on the plastic bench by the seaside, realising that she was dreaming while still inside her dream, she had felt so powerful, able to do anything; for the first time in her life, she had felt genuine hope. She thought she had grasped something, seen a light at the end of a tunnel. Light. That was what joined her waking consciousness and her sleeping mind. The light on her eyes, that familiar feeling of sleeping in the daytime and blinking uncontrollably in her dreams. If she can recreate that feeling in her sleeping body, she may be able to recreate that consciousness in her dreaming mind. But she cannot be too obvious about it; the four closed circuit cameras on the ceiling, if that's what they are, would register her unusual behaviour. Now more than ever she needs to be careful. Whatever you do, do not rock the boat.

She must continue to behave exactly in the same way, perform good behaviour for the cameras like she did for the telescreens when she was a free citizen. Tray of eggs, milk, and mushy oatmeal; tray of mashed potatoes and baked beans; tray of peas, gruel, and boiled meat. Pull your hair over your eyes, wait a few minutes lying still. Casually brush a hand over your face, as if tossing in your sleep, to brush the hair off of your closed eyelids, exposing them to the bright light. Falling asleep like this is hard, but Julia lies still for as long as she can, concentrating, trying to relax. The harder she tries, the less drowsy she feels. The screams of inmates being dragged to Room 101 get louder and louder in her head. The more she tries to block them out, the stronger they feel. All screaming of their terrifying experiences in the torture room.

How long have the other inmates been here, and what are they doing to them when they drag them out of their cubicles at night? What makes them scream of such fantastic occurrences? Are these people even real? Could she be hearing sounds played through amplifiers carefully positioned in the corridor to simulate movement? Julia has not seen or spoken to anyone since she was put in isolation. I did definitely see other inmates in the communal room, she muses. The idea that the entire Ministry of Love would be one massive fiction devised to terrify one person alone, and that I would be that person, is too far-fetched an endeavour even for Big Brother. No, I am not special, this place does not exist for me. I am just one among many. A disposable pawn. One that needs to be disposed of carefully, because before she ceased to be useful, she had been entrusted with a particu-larly sensitive task. What was it that O' Brien said? A project that the Party had invested valuable re-sources in.

That must be what awaits in Room 101: a punish-ment commensurate to the crime. The interminable postponement, the weeks in isolation, the daytime silence and the nocturnal cries, they are all a prelude to the time when guards will come and drag her to that room. What do they do to people there? Well, I sure as hell don't want to find out. I need to get to Sheila before they take me there. Sheila, oh Sheila, if only I could find you, I'm sure you would know what to do.

TWENTY-SEVEN.

Weeks go by as Julia tries to recreate her lucid dream experience. Careful not to modify her behaviour too conspicuously, she exercises a little harder to make herself tired, attempts breathing exercises to facilitate a deeper slumber, replays in her mind scenes from the place of glitter and music in the hope that it will resurface in her dreams. Her sleep is restless, her dreams fragmented and confused. Every night and every day a little piece of her is falling away. Toe the line and play their game; what else can she do?

How long have I been here? It was autumn when they caught us; it must be winter now. I have had my period twice since I've been in this cell. So it must be a little over two months. Has the winter solstice passed already? In the old days, it is around this time that people celebrated the capitalist festivity they called Christmas. Julia has read about it in textbooks. Exploited workers were forced to spend all their meagre income purchasing useless goods especially produced for this ritual exchange of gifts, lining the pockets of rich industrialists. Then at midnight of the chosen day they all attended a religious event called Mass, where they were promised rewards in a future life to compensate for the oppression and exploitation the capitalists subjected them to in this one.

The textbook said this was one of the core strategies deployed by capitalists to grow both their power and their wealth. They took their own celebration very seriously. The industrialists' Christmas was an opulent display of affluence. They commemorated the end of another year of capitalism by popping oversized bottles of champagne and eating enormous amounts of food, and made their servants work all night long to clean up, feeding them their half-chewed leftovers the next day. The detail about the leftovers always made teachers red with indignation when they taught about this feature of capitalist history.

Like with the top hats, Julia had always wondered whether the capitalist festivity of Christmas was as bad as it was portrayed in schoolbooks. Were workers really forced to give away all their wages to enrich the industrialists even further? What was the ritual exchange of gifts like? Did they get to keep the gifts after they exchanged it, or were those, too, stolen from them by the greedy capitalists? Even if that were the case, did they enjoy exchanging gifts? Was there a pleasure in the act of giving and receiving? But of course, I will never know; our only access to the history before the revolution is in the accounts of the

Party, and we know those accounts are largely made of lies.

Worn out by yet another restless night and lost in her thoughts, Julia does not hear the footsteps in the corridor, the cell door slamming open. When a booming voice resounds in the narrow space of the cubicle, she jolts from her bed, instinctively standing to attention.

"Come with us, Comrade Unwhite."

Julia doesn't know whether she is supposed to speak to the guards or not; she decides to keep her mouth shut, and they seem to appreciate it. They walk in silence along the brightly lit corridor. The white walls are lined with rows of identical white metal doors; the white ceiling is lined with rows of identical neon lights, that throw dark shadows at the guards' feet. The white cement floor feels rough under the thin soles of Julia's slippers. She is reminded of another walk along a corridor, with a similar tight knot in her stomach, a similar terror crawling under her skin. And yet everything in O' Brien's house was soft and smooth; she remembers the plush carpet and the creamy shine of wooden furniture under the dim, warm lights. It feels like a lifetime ago. A different Julia, a different world.

At the end of the long corridor, there is another long corridor. The guards march in silence, and Julia knows better than to ask how much longer it will be. Besides, it is nice to be able to stretch her legs after so many weeks in that cramped chamber. And then suddenly it is there, in front of her eyes, painted in large black characters. Room 101. As soon as they reach it, a door slides open, as if sensing their presence.

The inside of Room 101 is not much different from Julia's cell. The walls and ceiling are painted white; a cot in one corner, a toilet in another, four cameras in the ceiling, strategically positioned. No telescreens. For a moment, Julia has the dizzying feeling of having just walked in circles, returning to her starting point. Are they playing games with my mind?

"We are not playing games, Comrade."

O' Brien's voice seems to come from nowhere and everywhere at once; it fills the room; it fills her head. Is she supposed to answer out loud, if he is listening to her thoughts?

"That is an interesting question, Comrade. But I must reiterate, once again, that we are not playing games here. This is no time for speculating on trivial issues."

"Why am I here?"

"You know very well why you are here, Comrade. You deceived your Party and betrayed the trust that Big Brother had placed in you."

"Why am I in this room? What will happen to me here?"

"You are being given an opportunity to make amends, Comrade. An opportunity to embrace the love of Big Brother."

"How do I show my love for Big Brother?"

"You don't need to show your love for Big Brother, Comrade. You need to embrace Big Brother's love for you. The love that you rejected with your deception.

Are you ready to accept it now? Are you ready to put your full trust in the Party?"

"I am!"

Julia's voice is a strangled cry. Can it be this easy? Just say that you're sorry? It cannot be this simple. What do they really want?

"What is your occupation, Comrade Unwhite?"

"I am a level B step 4 operative in the Fiction Department in the Ministry of Truth. I have been a novel-making machinist since 1980. Before that, between 1978 and 1980, I worked for two years as an assistant photocopy operator in the News Department of the same ministry."

"Incorrect, Comrade. You are a level C step 5 operative in the kitchen department of the Ministry of Peace. You have been in that role since 1970."

"Er… I was born in 1958, so that's kind of impossible?"

Is this a mistaken identity case? Could she just be the victim of a bureaucratic error? Maybe there is hope after all: she can clarify the mistake and be released?

"Incorrect, Comrade. You have been an operative in the kitchen department of the Ministry of Peace since 1970."

"I am not! I don't have documents to prove it, but there must be a way… I only ever worked in the Ministry of Truth. I have never been at the Ministry of Peace. Comrade O' Brien, you… you were my… you were my supervisor, remember? You must remember that we… worked together? I mean, that I worked for your department?"

"Incorrect, Comrade. You have been an operative in the kitchen department of the Ministry of Peace since 1970."

What is going on here? What is the right answer? O'Brien seems to really want her to pretend to be this kitchen helper person. So be it. Toe the line, Julia, toe the line. It has saved you so many times: could it save you now too?

"My apologies, Comrade. You are correct. My name is Julia Unwhite, I am a level C step 5 operative in the kitchen department of the Ministry of Peace, and I have been in this role since 1970."

"Incorrect, Comrade. You are a level D step 1 operative in the carpentry department in the Ministry of Plenty, and you have been in that role since 1965."

"O... kay? I am?"

"Are you, Comrade?"

"I am! I am!"

"Are you really, Comrade? Do you genuinely believe that this is who you are?"

"I am. I do."

"You are who the Party says you are, Comrade. We all are who the Party says we are. Do you believe this? Do you really embrace this truth, from the bottom of your heart?"

"I do! I do! I swear..."

"Tell me about your work at the Ministry, then. What do you do there? Can you remember the last task you performed?"

"I..."

"You cannot remember that, can you? The memories are not there. You don't really believe that this is who you are, do you? You are still trying to deceive us, Comrade. You are not embracing Big Brother's truth with all your heart."

"But how can I do so? We cannot remember what didn't happen!"

"Yes, we can, Comrade. Yes we can."

"Please, just tell me what you want me to say and I will say it. I lied, I admit it. I will not lie anymore. Ever again. I swear it. Just help me. Please."

"We will, Comrade. This is why you are here. So that we can help you embrace Big Brother's truth. So that we can help you embrace Big Brother's love."

TWENTY-EIGHT.

"Do you remember when you were a child, Comrade, and you were taken on a school excursion to the Tower Bridge?"

Julia remembers this all too well; it was a freezing winter morning, and they all climbed up the tower, shivering. As they reached the glass floor, the other children were excited, but she was not able to move one foot. Frozen with terror, she stayed behind, forfeiting the most interesting part of the outing. As a result, she received a poor score on her report on the school trip, the only bad grade she received in all of her school years. But more than the embarrassment and the disappointment, it was the sheer terror of that glass floor, the dizzying depth underneath it, that still burned in Julia's memory. How do they know? But of course, they know everything. There must have been a report on this somewhere. Fear of heights is a potentially serious weakness if someone wants to join the military or become a firefighter, for example. More importantly, it could have been a sign of a more serious character flaw, such as laziness or cowardliness. Party schools meticulously recorded all of a child's shortcomings, to better monitor them in their adolescence and adulthood.

"And the Ministry of Love takes great interest in those records too. We want to know you well, Comrade, so that we can better help you."

As O' Brien speaks, the floor tiles begin to quiver under Julia's feet. Looking down, she sees a fissure opening to her left; the entire floor is moving, revealing a chasm several metres deep. Julia averts her gaze, vertigo already making her nauseous. Just as she shifts her feet to the right, moving away from the gap, another crevice opens on that side, about thirty centimetres from the first one. Planting her feet firmly, Julia glimpses a third gap forming in front of her. Too scared to look behind her, Julia feels certain that a fourth chasm has opened on that side. She is standing on a square tile barely larger than her two feet, surrounded on all sides by a thirty-metre deep precipice. Cold sweat runs down her back; her chest tightens and her throat closes. She is both shivering uncontrollably and unable to move a muscle; both freezing cold and burning hot. Paralysed with fear, she closes her eyes. And then it happens: the ringing in her ears grows both louder and smoother, turns into a familiar sound. The reddish darkness inside her eyelids grows deeper and brighter, turns into a familiar colour.

Julia opens her eyes and breathes deeply. The salty and damp air feels delicious. It must indeed be December; a chill wind bites her cheeks, and puffs of white steam come out of her mouth as she breathes out. The sky is overcast, the evening light fading, but rows of tiny lamps are strung across the street, casting blotches of yellow, red, and green on the people walking underneath them. A cheerful music, as upbeat as a military march but somehow more mellow, punctuated with silvery tones like small bells ringing, is being broadcast throughout the street. Yet there are no telescreens in sight; where could it be coming from?

Julia takes a few uncertain steps, and another tune, louder and with a faster tempo, floods her ears. This one is coming from a large black box with a loudspeaker encased in it. People are gathering around it; in their middle, a young man with a white helmet and white gloves is holding a life-size puppet donning the same outfit. Man and puppet both move to the rhythm of the music, jerking their arms and legs at sharp angles, as if they were being pulled by invisible strings. More people gather and start clapping to the sound of the music; when the tune changes, a young woman jumps into the circle and throws herself on the ground, arms and legs up in the air, gyrating on her back. She is wearing a black blouse and light grey trousers. The pants are so tight fitting that they look like a second skin; above them she has donned thick galoshes of a fluffy material, that cover only her shins, leaving her muscular thighs and buttocks exposed. As she whirls faster and faster, she extends one arm and her whole body rises pivoting on her hand, as if she were a spinning top. What are these people doing? Are they being tortured by invisible police? Has she escaped O' Brien's torture only to meet an even more dreadful fate?

"Wow, that's a sombre face! Don't you like break-dancing?"

Julia looks around, trying to locate the source of this utterance. Is she hearing voices in her head again? But a quick glance down reassures her; it is a child, maybe ten years old, standing right next to her in the crowd.

"Is that what they are doing? Breakdancing?"

"Duh! Of course they are. They come here every Monday. They are pretty cool. My brother does it sometimes too. He says I'm too young, but I wanna try it sometime. You've never seen breakdancing?" the child chuckles. Her eyes twinkle under her fluffy white hat; they are not the eyes of a spy. Julia has never seen such innocent eyes, if not perhaps in very small babies. Innocence may not be the right word; there is a cheekiness in the child's smirk, but it is not one that elicits alarm. This girl is so different from Juvenile Spies; she seems just a young person genuinely amused, and a little excited, that she knows more than someone twice her age.

"No, I have never seen it before. It looks quite wonderful."

"Hahaha, wow, you are strange, lady! Where are

you from?"

"I am from London."

"No, but where are you really from?"

"What do you mean? I am really from London. I work at the Ministry of Truth, in the Fiction Department."

The child's face suddenly turns serious, her eyes glowing with a new excitement.

"Come with me," she says, sweetly but firmly. There is something in her voice that commands respect; Julia follows her without asking questions. The child takes Julia's hand into her own small hand, and walks at a steady pace, fending the crowd of spectators. When they reach the other side of the circle, the girl suddenly stops and gestures towards the opposite sidewalk. Julia looks around her, unsure what she is supposed to be searching for. She spots a woman in a puffy black jacket and a bright red skirt, waving hands covered in gloves of the same bright red colour; is this what the childing is pointing to?

And then, she is right in front of her. Smiling at her. Reaching her arms towards her. Julia falls into Sheila's embrace, feels strong arms holding her at the waist, a warm mouth eagerly reaching for hers. It is a majestic kiss; long, joyous, soothing. It feels like coming home and it feels like starting on an exciting journey. A wave of relief washes over Julia; her knees buckle under her and she almost falls to the ground.

"My dear, you faint a bit too often, don't you think?"

Sheila's voice vibrates with the same happiness

Julia feels in every cell of her body.

"It's so good to see you, dear. I'm so glad you made it back here."

"I tried for so long, Sheila! I attempted everything. I wanted to dream my way back here so badly, but the harder I tried, the more it eluded me. I don't even know how I managed to get here this time!"

Sheila laughs. "It was them. They helped you get here."

"They did? What they were saying about helping me was true?" Julia cannot believe her ears.

"No, silly. Of course those pigs did not actually want to help you. They wanted you to surrender totally; they wanted to shock you into submission. They tortured you, didn't they?"

"Yes. They know your deepest fears. Apparently they keep records of all the instances where people exhibited horror of something, ever since childhood. And then they rely on those records to select the most effective forms of torture for thought criminals."

"What was yours?"

Julia shivers at the memory. "A fear of heights. It was absolutely terrifying."

"Oh, darling. That sounds really awful. I am so sorry. But I am also so glad that it brought you here."

"But how is that possible? Why did the torture bring me here? What do you mean, they helped me?"

"They didn't mean to help you, of course, but that's what they did. The result of the torture they inflicted on you was not the one they desired. I told you, they don't control everything. They think that they do, but things are more complex than they imagine. Those experiments that the Party has been conducting with dreams, they thought they would enable them to gain access to people's hearts. Compliance was not enough for Big Brother. He wanted genuine devotion. But things went very differently."

Sheila smiles at Julia and releases her from her tight embrace. They start walking towards the seaside, arm in arm.

"The Party has been experimenting with consciousness and dreams for many years. Initially they were cautious, but as time went by the experiments became bolder, reckless. And that's when things began to escape their control. You are not the first one to be shocked into a dream by these psychological tortures. The jolt caused by the fear is so intense that the mind is propelled all the way here."

"But what is this place? Am I really here? Am I dreaming?"

"You are here, Julia. Look at me. Do I seem real to you?"

"Very much so. This feels more real than anything I have lived in the past three months. Hell, it feels more real than my whole life."

"Exactly. You have come to the other side; you are here now."

"But won't I wake up? Every time I dreamed of this place, eventually I woke up back in... that other world."

"And every time you were in that other world,

eventually you came back here, didn't you? Even when you had given up hope, you made it back here. All you have to do now is remain here; stop moving back and forth, but do it from this side, not that one. Stay, Julia. The Party may want to conquer this world, they may want to drag you back to the Ministry of Love, but we will not let them. Please stay here. Don't dream it's over."

They have reached the shore; it is dark now, just like the first time they met on the beach. It is much colder than that day; the ocean breeze stings the two women's flushed faces. They gaze out at the black water, speckled with orange and white reflections.

"But for now, my dear, how about we just go back to my place and put a bottle of bubbly on ice before midnight?"

"Why midnight? What happens at midnight?"

"We celebrate New Year's Eve, silly. Come this way, let's go home. 1985 is going to be a great year."

ACKNOWLEDGE-MENTS

My thanks to Bruce Stronach, Alessandra Vota, and Olivier Ansart, who at different times read drafts of *Miniluv* and provided valuable criticism and advice. I am also grateful to the editorial team at RealMatter for their proofreading and formatting suggestions. Finally, my thanks to Thomas Campi for the wonderful cover art. All errors are of course mine.

ABOUT THE AUTHOR

Rebecca Suter

Rebecca Suter is associate professor at the University of Sydney, Australia, where she teaches and researches in Japanese and Comparative Literature. She also translates Japanese comics, novels, and nonfiction works.

BOOKS BY THIS AUTHOR

The Japanization Of Modernity: Murakami Haruki Between Japan And The United States

Holy Ghosts: The Christian Century In Modern Japanese Fiction

Rewriting History In Manga: Stories For The Nation

Women's Manga In Asia And Beyond

Two-World Literature: Kazuo Ishiguro's Early Novels

COPYRIGHT